Praise for *After the Fall, Before the Fall, During the Fall*

"An ecological apocalypse so real that it's like a three-dimensional object that can be viewed from all sides."
—Ted Kosmatka, author of *The Games*

"Nancy Kress displays all her usual strengths in *After the Fall, Before the Fall, During the Fall*: strong plotting, fast-paced action, complex and interesting characters, thought-provoking speculation. But there's something more here: a beautiful meditation on the fate of the earth, an elegy, a warning—and a glimpse of hope."
—Lisa Goldstein, author of *The Red Magician* and *The Uncertain Places*

"This is Nancy Kress in top form, but more importantly, this is SF done right. Here are big ideas about the environment and the future of humanity, married to an intimate story of family, community, and motherhood. With aliens and time travel to boot! I don't know of another writer who balances the global and the personal with such skill. I inhaled this story, and was sorry for it to end."
—Daryl Gregory, author of *Unpossible* and *The Devil's Alphabet*

"This story, of the terrible choices people must make in the face of ecological catastrophe, asks wrenching questions—*What does it take to remain human? What is survival worth?*—and answers with the authority that Kress always brings to bear on both science and humanity."
—Nicola Griffith, author of *Slow River* and *Always*

"The book is typical Kress, which means impossible to put down. A gripping tale of human survival."
—Jack McDevitt, author of *Infinity Beach* and *Echo*

"*After the Fall, Before the Fall, During the Fall* is the coming of age story for the human race. Nancy Kress has written a chillingly plausible tale of the end of the world."
—Mary Robinette Kowal, author of *Shades of Milk and Honey*

After the Fall, Before the Fall, During the Fall
© 2012 by Nancy Kress

Cover & interior design by Elizabeth Story

Tachyon Publications
1459 18th Street #139
San Francisco, CA 94107
415.285.5615

www.tachyonpublications.com
tachyon@tachyonpublications.com
smart science fiction & fantasy

Series Editor: Jacob Weisman
Editor: Marty Halpern
Project Editor: Jill Roberts

ISBN 13: 978-1-61696-065-0
ISBN 10: 1-61696-065-5

First Edition: 2012

Printed in the United States of America by Worzalla

9 8 7 6 5 4 3 2 1

AFTER
THE FALL
BEFORE
THE FALL
DURING
THE FALL

TACHYON / SAN FRANCISCO

NOVEMBER 2013

I T WASN'T DARK, and it wasn't light. It wasn't anything except cold. *I'm dead*, Pete thought, but of course he wasn't. Every time he thought that, all the way back to his first time when McAllister had warned him: *"The transition may seem to last forever."*

Forever was twenty seconds on Pete's wrister.

Light returned, light the rosy pink of baby toes, and then Pete stood in a misty dawn. And gasped.

It was so *beautiful*. A calm ocean, smooth and shiny as the floor of the Shell. A beach of white sand, rising in dunes dotted with clumps of grasses. Birds wheeled overhead. Their sharp, indignant cries grew louder as one of them dove into the waves and came up with a fish. Just like that. A fresh breeze tingled Pete's nose with salt.

This. All this. He hadn't landed near the ocean before, although he'd seen pictures of it in one of Caity's books. *This*—all destroyed by the Tesslies, gone forever.

No time for hatred, not even old hatred grown fat and ripe as soy plants on the farm. McAllister's instructions, repeated endlessly to all of them, echoed in Pete's mind: *"You have only ten minutes. Don't linger anywhere."*

The sand slipped under his shoes and got into the holes. He had to leave them, even though shoes were so hard to come by. Cursing, he ran clumsy and barefoot along the shoreline, his weak knee already aching and head bobbing on his spindly neck, toward the lone house emerging from the mist. The cold air seeped into his lungs and hurt them. He could see his breath.

Seven minutes remained on his wrister.

The house stood on a little rocky ridge rising from the dunes and jutting into the water. No lights in the windows. The back door was locked but McAllister had put their precious laser saw onto the wrister. (*"If you lose it, I will kill you."*) Pete cut a neat, silent hole, reached in, and released the deadbolt.

Five minutes.

Dark stairs. A night light in the hallway. A bedroom with two sleeping forms, his arm thrown over her body, the window open to the sweet night air. Another bedroom with a single bed, the blanketed figure too long, shadowy clothes all over the floor. And at the end of the hallway, a bonanza.

Two of them.

Four minutes.

The baby lay on its back, eyes closed in its bald head, little pink mouth sucking away on dreams. It had thrown off its blanket to expose a band of impossibly smooth skin between the plastic diaper and tiny shirt. Pete took precious seconds to unfasten a corner of the diaper, but he was already in love with the little hairless creature and would have been devastated if it were male. It was a girl. Carefully he hoisted her out of the crib and onto his shoulder, painfully holding her with one crooked arm. She didn't wake.

No doubt that the toddler was a girl. Glossy brown ringlets, pink pajamas printed with bunnies, a doll clutched in one chubby fist. When Pete reached for her, she woke, blinked, and shrieked.

"No! Mommy! Dada! Cooommme! No!"

Little brat!

Pete grabbed her by the hand and dragged her off the low bed. That wrenched his misshapen shoulder and he nearly screamed. The child resisted, wailing like a typhoon. The baby woke and also screamed. Footsteps pounded down the hall.

Ninety seconds.

"McAllister!" Pete cried, although of course that did no good. McAllister couldn't hear him. And ten minutes was fixed by the Tesslie machinery: no more, no less. McAllister couldn't hurry the Grab.

The parents pounded into the room. Pete couldn't let go of either child. Pete shrieked louder than both of them—his only real strength was in his voice, did they but know it—the words Darlene had taught him: "Stop! I have a bomb!"

They halted just inside the bedroom door, crashing into each other. She gasped: perhaps at the situation, perhaps at Pete. He knew what he must look like to them, a deformed fifteen-year-old with bobbly head.

"Moommmeeeee!" the toddler wailed.

"Bomb! Bomb!" Pete cried.

Forty-five seconds.

The father was a hero. He leaped forward. Pete staggered sideways with his burden of damp baby, but he didn't let go of the toddler's hand. Her father grabbed at her torso and Pete's wrister shot a laser beam at him. The man was moving; the beam caught the side of his arm. The air sizzled with burning flesh and the father let go of his child.

But for only a few precious seconds.

Now the mother rushed forward. Pete dodged behind the low bed, nearly slipping on a pillow that had fallen to the floor. Both of them sprang again, the man's face contorted with pain, and clutched at their children. Pete fired the laser but his hold on the child had knocked the wrister slightly sideways and he missed. Frantically he began firing, the beams hitting the wall and then Pete's own foot. The pain was astonishing. He screamed; the children screamed; the mother screamed and lunged.

Five seconds.

The father tore the little girl from Pete. Pete jerked out his bad arm, now in as much pain as his foot, as much pain as the man's must be, and twined his fingers in the child's hair. The mother slipped on a throw rug patterned with princesses and went down. But the father held on to the toddler and so did Pete, and—

Grab.

All four of them went through in a blaze of noise,

of light, of stinking diapers and roasted flesh, of shoulder pain so intense that Pete had to struggle to stay conscious. He did, but not for long. Once under the Shell, he collapsed to the metal floor. The father, of course, was dead. The last thing Pete heard was both children, still wailing as if their world had ended.

It had. From now on, they were with him and McAllister and the others. From now on, poor little devastated parentless miracles.

MARCH 2014

ON THE HIGH PLATEAU of the Brazilian state of Paraná, the arabica trees rustled in a gentle rain. Drops pattered off dark green, lance-shaped leaves, cascading down until they touched the soil. The coffee berries were small, not ready for harvest until the dry season, months away. At the far edge of the vast field, a fertilizer drove slowly among the rows of short, bushy trees, some of them fifty years old. A rabbit raced ahead of the advancing machinery.

Deep underground, something happened.

Nonmotile, rod-shaped bacteria clung to the roots of the coffee trees, as they had for millennia. The bacteria stuck to the roots by exuding a slime layer, where it fed on and decomposed plant matter into nutrients. In the surrounding soil other bacteria also flourished, carrying on their usual life processes. One of these was mitosis. During the reproductive division, plasmids were swapped between organisms, as widely promiscuous as all of their kind.

A new bacterium appeared.

Eventually it, too, began to divide, not too rapidly in the dry soil. By and by, another plasmid exchange took place, with a different bacterium. And so on, in an intricate chain, ending up with a plasmid swap with the nonmotile, rod-shaped root dweller. A mutation now existed that had never existed before. Such a thing happened all the time in nature—but not like this.

Above ground, thunder rumbled, and the rain began to fall harder.

NOVEMBER 2013

THE WOMAN was hysterical. *As she had every right to be,* Julie thought. Julie laid her hand across her own belly, caught herself doing it, and removed the hand. Quickly she glanced around. No one had noticed. They all watched the woman, and all of them, even the female uniform, had the expressions that cops wore in the presence of hysterical victims: a mixture of stern pity and impatient disgust.

"Ma'am...ma'am...if you could just calm down enough to tell us what happened..."

"I told you! I told you!" The woman's voice rose to a shriek. She wore a gaping bathrobe over a flimsy white nightdress, and her hair was so wild it looked as if she had torn out patches by the roots, like some grieving Biblical figure. Perhaps she had. A verse from Julie's unwilling Temple childhood rose, unbidden, in her mind: *"In Rama was there a voice heard, lamentation, and weeping, and great mourning, Rachel weeping for her children, and would not be comforted, because they were no more."*

"Ma'am...shit. Get a doctor here with a sedative," the "detective" said. He was a captain in this seaside town's police. Julie had picked up from Gordon an

FBI agent's contempt for local law enforcement; she would have to rid herself of that, or else turn into as much of a machine as Gordon could be. She stepped forward.

"May I try?"

"No." The captain glared; he hadn't wanted her along in the first place. They never did. Julie stepped back into the shadows. Gordon would be here soon.

The woman continued to wail and tear her hair. A uniform phoned for a doctor. In the bedroom the forensics team worked busily, and through the window Julie could see men fanning out across the beach, looking for clues. Had this mother drowned her infants? Buried them? Hidden them safe in baskets of bulrushes, a crazy latter-day Jochebed with two female versions of Moses? Julie knew better. She studied the room around her.

Simple, classic North Atlantic beach cottage: white duck covers on the wicker furniture, sisal mats on the floor, light wood and pale colors. But the house had central heating and storm windows already in place; evidently the family lived here year-round. Bright toys spilled from a colorful box. Beside the sofa, a basket of magazines, *TIME* shouting: CAN THE PRESIDENT CONTROL CONGRESS? and THE DESERTIFICATION OF AFRICA. On the counter separating the kitchen from the living area, a homemade pie under a glass dome, next to a pile of fresh tomatoes, onions, zucchini. Everything orderly, prosperous, caring.

Gordon strode through the door and went unerringly to the detective. "Captain Parsons? I'm Special

Agent in Charge Gordon Fairford. We spoke on the phone."

Parsons said sourly, "No change from what I told." On the sofa, the woman let out another air-splitting wail.

"What do you think happened, Captain?" Gordon said. Whatever his private opinion, Gordon was always outwardly tactful with locals, who always resented both the tact and the FBI involvement. The eternal verities.

Parsons said, "The husband took the kids, of course. Or they disposed of them together and he took a powder."

"Any signs of his leaving, with or without them?"

"No," Parsons said, with dislike.

Nor would there be, Julie thought. Gordon went on extracting as much information from Parsons as he could, simultaneously smoothing over as much as possible of the inevitable turf war. Julie stopped listening. She waited until Parsons moved off and Gordon turned to her.

He said, "This time your location forecast was closer."

"Not close enough." If it had been, Gordon would have been at the beach house before the kids' disappearance happened. As it was, he and she had only managed to be in the next town over. Not enough, not nearly enough.

The woman on the couch had quieted slightly. Gordon said softly to Julie, "Go."

This was never supposed to be part of her job. She

was the math wizard, the creator of algorithms, the transformer of raw data into useful predictions. But she and Gordon had been working closely together for over six months now, and he had discovered her other uses.

No, no, not what I meant!

Julie sat next to the sobbing woman, without touching her. "Mrs. Carter, I'm Julie Kahn. And I know you're telling the truth about what happened to your husband and children."

The woman jerked as if she had been shot and fastened both hands on Julie's arm. Her nails dug in, and her eyes bored silently into Julie's face, wider and wilder than any eyes Julie had ever seen. She tried not to flinch.

Julie said, "There was a flash of light when they were taken, wasn't there? Very bright. Almost blinding."

"Yes!"

"Tell me everything, from the beginning."

"Can you get them back? Can you? Can you?"

No. "I don't know."

"You must get them back!"

"We'll do what we can. Was it a short teenage boy with a wobbling head, as if the head were too big for his neck? Or was it a girl?"

Mrs. Carter shuddered. "It was a demon!"

Oh. It was going to be like that.

"A demon from Hell and he has Jenny and Kara!" She began to wail again and tear her hair.

Slowly, painfully, Julie extracted the story. It

wasn't much different from the others, except that this time there had been two children, and the husband had disappeared, too. Apparently he had been hanging onto one of the kids. Was that significant?

How did you know what was significant when it was all unthinkable?

Eight other children in the last year, all vanished without a trace, each taken from a different town on the Atlantic coast. Only three of the abductions had been witnessed, however, and one of those had not succeeded. The mother had beaten off the kidnapper—a young girl—before the perp vanished in a dazzlingly bright light. Or so the mother said. But children disappeared all the time, which is why the press had not yet gotten the larger story. But even the unwitnessed disappearances followed a pattern, and patterns were what Julie did. There were other incidents, too: mostly thefts from locked stores. She was less sure those fitted, and her algorithms had to weight for that. But the geographical pattern was there, if bizarrely nonlinear, and what kind of kidnapper was both smart enough to plan ten flawless abductions and stupid enough to leave any signature at all in their geography?

Julie was not law enforcement. Gordon was, and they had discussed the question endlessly over the last months. Gordon's answer: *A psycho who wants to be caught.*

Julie had no answers. Only terrible fears.

"It was a demon! A demon!" Mrs. Carter suddenly shrieked. "I want Ed and my kids back!" She tore out of the dune cottage, robe flapping and hair whipping around her ravaged face, as if she could find her husband and children on the cold beach. A cop leaped after her; she was of course a suspect.

Julie wiped the blood off her arm where Mrs. Carter's nails had pierced the skin. Did that mean she needed a tetanus shot? Was a tetanus shot even safe for her now?

She crossed her arms over her belly and closed her eyes. When she opened them again, Gordon stood watching her.

APRIL 2014

THE SUN ROSE above the salt marsh on the Connecticut coast. The tide flowed gently out, toward the barrier island that sheltered the land. A light breeze ruffled the cordgrass, although the breeze was not strong enough to cause waves on the pearly water. A blue heron did disturb the water, landing on a mudflat to dip its long bill, searching for breakfast. A sea-pink bloomed on a raised hummock, turning its dome-shaped cluster of flowers toward the sun.

In the mud beside the heron's long thin toes, something changed.

Bacteria sliming the roots of cordgrass swapped plasmids with another species, the result of a long and intricate chain of such exchanges. The new bacteria began to feed. Abruptly, it died, unable in this mutated form to tolerate the high salt content of brackish marsh.

The heron rose and flew away into the dawn.

2035

IT TOOK PETE days and days to recover from the laser burn on his foot, which became infected. McAllister was out of her special medicine—"antibiotics," Pete thought it was called—because one of the Grab kids had needed the last dose. Sometimes McAllister sat beside Pete, sometimes Paolo and once Caity, but usually no one tended him. No one could be spared.

He came to loathe his tiny, bare "bedroom" with no bed, just a pile of blankets on the floor and a shit bucket in the corner. Why hadn't he taped something to the wall like Caity did in her room—something, anything to look at? They still had some tape left. Caity had taped up a picture that one of the children tore out of a precious book, a girl riding a big black horse, and beside it a bright piece of patterned cloth from an old Grab. All Pete had to look at was white Tesslie-metal walls, white Tesslie-metal ceiling, white Tesslie-metal floor.

He drifted in and out of sleep that never refreshed him. When his fever rose high enough he thought he saw other rooms around him: The impossibly gorgeous, rich bedroom from which he'd taken the

19

round-headed baby that Bridget had named Kathleen. The ugly city apartment with stained and crumbling walls where he'd found Tina, alone in her bed except for the rat attracted by the milk around her unwiped little mouth. The strange house, decorated only with bright pillows and low, silver-inlaid tables where he'd snatched dark, curly-haired Karim, whose name he knew only because his mother had screamed it just before Pete pushed her down that short flight of stairs to get away. Those other rooms rose around him, shimmered on the air like the world he'd seen only in snatches on Grabs, and then collapsed into so much rubble.

"Sleep, Pete." McAllister, a cool hand on his forehead. Or maybe not, because McAllister collapsed, too, but into a shimmer of golden sparks. Like the Tesslie that McAllister described in learning circles! Pete struggled to sit up.

"No! No...not you...Tessl...."

"Sleep."

When he woke for the last time from fever and delirium, he was alone.

Cautiously he got himself up off the pallet of blankets. Pete recognized them; he'd brought them back himself, from his first store Grab. They needed washing. Everything needed washing, including himself. But that could wait.

He lurched dizzily to the door. A Grab was supposed to be painless, and usually it was. But you weren't supposed to shoot your own foot! Still, everyone took risks during Grabs, or at least everyone who could still go. Look what had happened to Caity on her last Grab: that mother had beat Caity off, breaking her arm, and Caity hadn't even been strong enough to keep the child. McAllister was thinking of taking Caity off Grab duty, which would leave just Pete, Ravi, and Paolo to do them all, at least until Terrell turned twelve. Anyway, it was better than shit-bucket duty.

Pete's room opened onto the corridor that ran the whole half-mile length of the egg-shaped Shell. Each end of the corridor branched into maybe a hundred of these tiny rooms. The Survivors and the Six used some of them at the living end as bedrooms, and McAllister had designated a few more as storage or work areas. None of the rooms at the far end of the Shell were used at all. In the center was the important stuff.

Such a long way to hobble. Below Pete's halting feet, one painful enough that finally he just hopped on the other and leaned against the wall for support, stretched the same featureless white metal as his room. Above curved the ceiling of the Shell, three times his height. On either side were doors, some open and some closed, leading to more tiny rooms, white metal walls. Tesslie stuff, all of it. Stuff preserving his life. Pete hated it.

Another hundred yards to the farm, the children's room, the Grab room.

All at once he didn't want to go to any of them. The children's room, spacious and always busy, would be cheerful with toys, learning circles, babies

21

cooing or wailing. Caity or Jenna or Terrell would be there, whoever was on duty. Someone would also be on duty with Darlene in the farm. Someone else would be watching—endlessly, boringly—the Grab machinery. Pete was sick of all of it. This time it had nearly gotten him killed. The only person he would have liked to see was McAllister, and he'd been sick so long that he'd lost track of the duty roster and had no idea where McAllister, or anybody else, might be now.

Miraculously unnoticed, Pete crept past the wide archways which opened on one side of the corridor to the children's room and on the other to the farm. From the farm came the smell of dirt and the fall of water in the disinfecting and clean-water streams. Also the clank of buckets; someone was on duty at the fertilizer machine. From the children's room came the usual babble, the playing and crying and talking of eight—no, now ten!—small children.

Head wobbling on his thin neck, he hopped past the smaller, doorless openings to the rooms holding Tesslie machinery and entered the maze of tiny, unused rooms at the far end of the Shell. His foot, wrapped in pieces of torn blanket, still hurt. "Stupid fucking foot!" McAllister had forbidden that word, but Pete—all of the Six—had learned a rich cursing vocabulary from Darlene. Her only useful contribution, in Pete's opinion, to life in the Shell. Mean old woman.

Finally he reached a small, low chamber at the very tip of the Shell. Here part of the outer wall was, for some reason, clear. Why had the Tesslies done that? But, then, why had they destroyed the world nearly twenty-one years ago and then chosen to imprison a handful of survivors? Nobody knew why the fucking bastards did anything. Pete sank to the metal floor and looked out.

There wasn't much to see: just a strip of land between him and where the ground curved abruptly away. That strip was a uniform expanse of empty black rock, once smooth but now starting to split in places. The rock had a name, and so did the thing the Shell sat on, but Pete didn't remember them. Basil? No, that was a prince in *The Illustrated Book of Fairy Tales*. Balit? Basalt? He'd never been good at learning such stuff, not like Jenna or Paolo. They were the smart ones. What Pete was good at was the Grab.

And hatred. He was terrific at hatred. So he gazed out at his tiny view of the vast dead world the Tesslies had killed, and thought about the beauty of the shore cottage where he had Grabbed the two children, and he hated.

APRIL 2014

DEEP BENEATH THE ICE pack of the Canadian glacier, the earth shifted. Basalt magma flowed into a chamber heavy with silica and the two mingled. From below, more magma pushed upward, exerting pressure. Above, glacial ice tens of thousands of years old but already thinned by global warming, gleamed under a cold spring sky.

NOVEMBER 2013

GORDON STOOD at one end of the table that was really two tables pushed together, one moved from the bedroom of the motel "suite." Julie stood at the other end, willing him to leave. The rest of the task force had already gone to their own rooms for the night, leaving Styrofoam cups with the remnants of cold coffee, empty pizza boxes, crumpled paper napkins, half-crushed beer cans. On the desk Julie's industrial-strength laptop, in sleep mode, glowed with a blue light.

It had been a bad idea to hold the team meeting in her room, but Gordon's wife, impelled by some marital crisis Julie wanted no part of, kept phoning his room after she'd been told not to call his cell. Maybe that was why he hadn't left yet; Deborah was a weeper. Or so Julie had been told. She didn't want to know for sure. If Gordon tried to talk personally with her now…

He didn't. He studied her latest printout, frowning at the equations as if he understood them. "So you think somewhere in Hingham, next Thursday?"

"That's what the algorithms say."

"God, Julie, I need a more specific location than that! Unless I can witness an actual kidnapping, maybe even have a camera set up—"

She held onto her temper. "I'm a mathematician, Gordon, not a magician. And I've given you everything I've got."

A second later, horror hit her at her own wording, but Gordon, frowning at the sheaf of papers, apparently hadn't noticed. That caused horror to give way to anger. He never had been any good at reading her feelings, had always enclosed himself in that "objective" professional shell. Well, let him.

He ran a hand over the gray stubble on his head. "I know. I didn't mean to snap. But funding for this task force is hanging by a thread. The A-Dic isn't convinced that the child abductions are linked, and he's never believed any of the witnesses, you know that."

"I know. Can't blame him, really." Two witnesses—no, three now, with Mrs. Carter—attesting that someone had invaded their homes, stolen or tried to steal a child, and then dissolved, child and all, into thin air, to the accompaniment of a burst of bright light. Twice the alleged intruder was a deformed teenage boy with a wobbly head, dressed in what was described as a blanket. Once it was a girl, who had been successfully fought off until she dematerialized. Who would believe any of that? Nor did it help that two of the women had been hysterical types; one was now in a mental institution. Some days Julie wasn't sure that she herself believed this stuff. The common MOs, yes. The irrefutable fact that the children were gone, yes. Above all, the algorithms that traced a nonlinear but discernible mathematical path for the kidnappings.

She said, "Your Assistant Director has reason to doubt. But I think my usefulness to the task force is pretty much over, and anyway Georgetown wants me back for the spring semester. I've booked a flight back to D.C. for tomorrow."

Gordon looked up. Was that relief in his eyes? She was lying about Georgetown, but he didn't know that. He said, "Will you stay on call if we have any questions?"

"Sure." She rose, which was a mistake. The wave of nausea took her by surprise, surging up her throat so suddenly that she barely made it to the bathroom. After she threw up, she kicked the door closed behind her, then took her time rinsing her mouth and brushing her teeth. By the time she came out, he would have gone.

He hadn't. He stood at the end of the table, papers crumpled in one hand, his still handsome face as white as the printouts. A little vein throbbed in his forehead. "My God, Julie."

"It's nothing. Something I ate at dinner."

"It's not." And then, "I have three kids, remember."

Something in her that she hadn't counted on, some streak of anger or blame, made her lash out at him. "Now you've got one more."

"Why didn't you *tell* me?"

She sat down. The motel chair creaked under her. "Let's get one thing straight, Gordon. This has nothing to do with you. I mean, it *will* have nothing to do with you. You don't need to be involved at all."

"You're keeping it?"

"Yes." She was thirty-eight, with no real relationship in sight now that the ill-thought-out thing with Gordon had ended. This might be her last chance.

"How far along are you?"

"Three and a half months." Her stocky figure meant that, with her habitually loose clothing, no one had yet noticed. They would soon. She had arranged to extend her sabbatical from Georgetown to a full year, had already bought a crib, a changing table, impossibly tiny onesies. The nausea was supposed to have stopped by now but, as her obstetrician said, every pregnancy is different.

Gordon's jaw tightened. "You weren't going to tell me at all, were you?"

"No." And then, from that same unexplored well of anger—but at what? "You have your hands full already, with Deborah and your kids."

They stared at each other for a long moment. Julie found herself studying him almost impersonally, as if he were someone she'd just met. Such a handsome man, with his deep blue eyes, firm jaw, prematurely gray hair that looked masterful rather than old. "Masterful"—that was the right word for Gordon. He liked to control situations. And yet he had been tender with her, from the conventional beginning of too-long "business dinners," through the trite progression to so much more.

Had she really ever loved him? It had felt like

romance, those first few months of delicious hidden hours. And yet even then, Julie had had her doubts. Not because Gordon was married, but because of something in his character and—be honest!—in her own. Both of them wanted to make their own decisions, keep their options open. That stubborn independence was why Julie had never married, and why Gordon cheated on his wife. Neither had ever told the other "I love you." Both had wanted freedom more than the inevitable compromises and sacrifices of genuine love.

And yet now Gordon stood at his end of the littered table, running his hand through his gray hair and looking more troubled than Julie had known possible. But, then, Gordon was not one to shirk responsibilities. That wouldn't have fit with his image of himself.

"Julie, if there's anything I can do...money..."

Her anger evaporated. This situation was not his fault. Nor hers—precautions sometimes failed. Gordon would never leave drama-queen Deborah, and she didn't want him to, no matter what romantic fantasies dictated that she should want. Julie needed nothing from him.

"I'm fine," she said gently. "Truly."

"At least let me—"

"No." She went into her motel bedroom and closed the door, her back to it until she heard him leave.

APRIL 2014

THE SHEEP PASTURE high in New Zealand hills lay thick in white clover. One corner of the pasture had been planted with chicory, but the clover grew wild. Low, white-flowered, sweet-smelling, it attracted the bees buzzing above the fenced pasture. Sheep munched contentedly, flicking their tails. Beside the fence, two lambs chased each other.

The clover's root system, fibrous and fast-growing, laced itself through the soil. The original tap root extended three feet deep; branches clustered thickly near the top grew, in turn, a mass of fine rootlets. Much of the system was slimed with new bacteria, created by a long chain of plasmid swaps. There had been more than enough candidates for this gene-swapping: a teaspoon of the sheep pasture's soil contained over 600 million bacteria. The new anaerobic strain included a gene that broke down carbohydrates, producing carbon dioxide and alcohol.

The alcohol accumulated on the plant roots. In a short time the fermentation had deposited ethanol on the plant roots in a concentration of one part per million. When the concentration reached twice that, the clover began to die.

The new bacteria went on multiplying. A ewe munched up a handful of clover, jostling the root system so that it touched another. The ewe ambled on toward her lamb.

2035

MCALLISTER DIDN'T LET PETE sit alone by the Shell wall for very long. She found him in another of the maze of unused rooms, as she always found him wherever he went, and knelt beside him. The folds of her simple long dress, made from a blue bed sheet patterned with yellow flowers, puddled on the metal floor. "Pete."

"Go away."

"No." She didn't put her arms around him; she knew better, after last time. He had hit her. From frustration, hurt, anger, hate. Never had he regretted anything so much in his short life.

"Then don't go away. I don't care."

She smiled. "Yes, you do. And I have something good to tell you."

Despite himself, he said, "What?"

"The two little girls you brought us a week ago are doing fine."

"They are?" And then, because he didn't want to look yet at anything good, "A *week* ago? I was sick for a week?"

"Yes."

"I missed a whole week of duties?"

"Yes, but don't worry about it. Your foot got infected and you were wonderful. Just kept fighting. You always do."

That was McAllister: always encouraging, always kind. She was one of the Survivors, from the time before the Tesslies destroyed the world. When that happened, McAllister had been only twenty-one, six years older than Pete was now. The Tesslies had put her and twenty-five others in the Shell, and then—what? Kept them there to breed and…. Pete didn't know what the Tesslies had wanted, or wanted now. Who could understand killer aliens who destroyed a world and then for over twenty years kept a zoo going with random survivors? And when that experiment failed, having produced only six children, replaced it with another experiment involving machinery that they could have put in the Shell decades before?

Only four of the Survivors were still alive: McAllister, Eduardo, Xiaobo, and the awful Darlene. "Radiation damage created cancers and genetic damage," McAllister had said; Pete hadn't listened closely to the rest of the explanation. Jenna and Paolo, not him, were good at that science stuff. What Pete knew was that the Survivors miscarried, got weaker, eventually died. Most of them he couldn't even remember, including both his biological parents, although he was the oldest of the Six. But he remembered Seth and Hannah, Robert and Jenny, and especially kind and loving Bridget, who had died only three months ago. All the Six had loved Bridget, and so had the Grab kids.

Pete looked at McAllister. She was so beautiful. Her face was lined and her breasts sagged a little beneath her loose dress, but her body was slim and curving, her dark eyes and rich brown skin unmarred. And she was whole. Not damaged like the next generation, the Six. Not old-looking like the other three Survivors. She was the smartest of everybody, and the sweetest. Again Pete felt the love surge up in him, and the lust. The latter was completely hopeless and he knew it. The knowledge turned him sullen again.

"So who did the next Grab? Was there one?"

"The platform brightened but nobody went."

"Why didn't Paolo go? He was next in line!"

"He fell asleep and missed it."

"He's a wimp." It was their deadliest insult, learned from the Survivors. It meant you shirked your fair share of work and risk and unpleasant duties like lugging shit buckets to the fertilizer machine. It was also unfair applied to Paolo, who had always been sickly and couldn't help falling asleep. He had some disease that made him do it. Pete had forgotten the name.

"Paolo isn't really strong enough for a Grab unless it's a store, and who can predict that?" McAllister said reasonably. "I'm taking him off Grab duty. Pete, don't you want to hear about the little girls?"

"No. Caity could have gone on the Grab when Paolo fell asleep," he said, although he knew that if it wasn't her turn, she wouldn't have been anywhere near the machinery. But Pete had his own reasons for a grudge against Caity, reasons he couldn't tell

McAllister. And the truth was that of the Six, Pete and Ravi were best at the Grab. Terrell wouldn't go until he turned twelve, Paolo and Jenna had gotten too sickly, Caity had her arm broken when she tried to Grab a child, which she hadn't even been able to bring back. Although, to be fair, Caity insisted on going again as soon as her arm healed. But Pete was in no mood to be fair to Caity.

Only the Six could go through the Grab machinery. Before the humans in the Shell knew that, they'd lost two Survivors, Robert and Seth. You'd think the Tesslies would have told McAllister about the age limit when they left the Grab machinery a year ago! But no one had even seen them leave the machinery (and how did they do that?). Nobody had seen a Tesslie in twenty-one years, and nobody ever had heard one speak. Maybe they couldn't.

McAllister said, still trying to cheer up Pete, "Both little girls are adjusting so much better than we'd hoped. You must come see them. The little girl said her name is Kara. She just called the infant 'Baby,' so we had to pick a name for her, and we chose 'Petra.' After you."

Petra. Despite himself, Pete rolled the name on his tongue, savoring it as once—only once—he'd savored "candy" that Paolo had Grabbed when he'd found himself sent to a store. They'd all had a piece. Reese's Peanut Butter Cups, McAllister had called them. Feeling the astounding sweetness dissolve on his tongue, Pete had hated the Tesslies all over again. This, this, *this*—he might have had a Reese's Peanut

Butter Cup every day of his life! A whole Peanut Butter Cup, every day!

He might even have had a woman like McAllister.

"Come see Petra," she coaxed.

He'd been trained since birth not to indulge himself. *Don't be a wimp!* Indulgence in moods was selfish and against the restarting of humanity. Some of the others might be better at remembering that—well, *all* of the others—but Pete had his pride. He'd been indulgent enough for one day. He got painfully to his feet, his head wobbling, and followed McAllister to see Petra.

APRIL 2014

THE CONNECTICUT SALT MARSH had been filled in during the 1940s, restored during the 1980s, overrun with too many tourists enjoying its beauty in the 1990s, and finally declared an ecologically protected area in 2004. Although it proved impossible to completely eliminate the invasive nonnative plant species, the natural floral layering of back-barrier marsh was returning. At the lowest level, where the tide brought surges of salt water twice a day, cordgrass and glassworts dominated. Higher up, it was salt hay. Higher still, on the upland border of the marsh, the ground was thick with black rush and marsh elder.

A particularly large marsh elder, nearly eight feet high, held a half-finished nest. A red-winged blackbird brought another piece of grass, laid it in the nest, and flew off. The shrub's still furled buds, which would soon become greenish-white flowers, bobbed in a wind from the sea.

Below ground, bacteria mutated again. This time it found the lower salinity much more congenial than it had the roots of cordgrass, a month ago. The bacterial slime engaged in all its metabolic processes, including mitosis and fermentation. Alcohol began to accumulate on the marsh elder's roots.

NOVEMBER 2013

JULIE SAT IN A CROWDED Starbucks in D.C. across the table from her best friend, Linda Campinelli. Julie's latte and Linda's double caramel macchiato sat untouched. The women known each other since Princeton, brought together by the vagaries of the roommate-matching computer even though they were complete opposites. Linda, a large untidy woman with a large untidy husband and three riotous sons, was an animal psychologist in Bethesda. She told long, funny stories about neurotically territorial cats or schnauzers that developed a fear of their water dishes. But not today.

"Ju…are you *sure?*"

"I'm four months along. Of course I'm sure."

"Gordon?"

"Of course it was Gordon! How many men do you think I was banging at once?"

"I meant what will Gordon and you *do?*"

Julie had expected this. Linda was not only a romantic, she was sociability squared. Maybe even cubed. Not even after four years of dorm living did Linda understand Julie's preference for silence and solitude. For Linda, all decisions and all endeavors were group activities.

"Linda, there is no 'Gordon and me.' And I don't want there to be. I'm having the baby, I'm keeping the baby, I'm raising the baby. Georgetown's given me a year's sabbatical, for which I was overdue anyway. I've got great medical coverage. I feel fine now that morning sickness is over. And I'm happy to be doing this alone."

"Except for me," said Linda, to whom anything else was unthinkable.

Julie smiled. "Of course. You can be my labor coach. Always good to have a coach who won all her own games."

"And your due date is—"

"May 1."

Linda sipped her caramel macchiato. Julie saw that her friend was still troubled. Linda would never understand isolates like Julie and Jake.

As if reading Julie's mind, Linda said, "And how is that gorgeous brother of yours?"

"Still monitoring mud in Wyoming." Jake was a geologist.

"What did he say about the baby?"

"I haven't told him yet."

"But he'll come here for the birth, right?"

"I'm sure he will," said Julie, who was sure of no such thing. She and Jake liked being affectionate at a distance.

"Then you'll have me and Jake, and I'm sure that Lucy Anderson will come to—"

Ah, Linda! Even parturition required a committee.

That evening Julie's cell rang just as she was tapping the lid back on a paint can in her D.C. apartment. Paint had spilled over the side of the can and flowed down its side, but fortunately she had laid down a thick wad of paper. Winterfresh green puddled over a science article: POLLUTION FROM ASIA CONTAMINATES STRATOSPHERE. Julie's paper mask was still in place; the baby book had recommended a filter mask if a pregnant woman felt it absolutely necessary to paint something. Julie had felt it absolutely necessary to paint her mother's old chest of drawers, after which she would apply decals of bears. The ultrasound showed she was having a girl. But no Disney princesses or any of that shit; Julie's daughter would be brought up to be a strong, independent woman. Bears were a good start.

The nursery, formerly Julie's study, was very cold, since the baby book had also recommended painting with open windows. She shivered as she picked up her cell and walked into the hallway of the two-bedroom apartment, squeezing past the furniture and boxes moved from her former study. Somehow she would have to find room for all this stuff. At the moment her computer and printer sat on the dining table and her file cabinet crowded the kitchen. The baby wasn't even here yet and it had disrupted everything. "Hello. Julie Kahn speaking."

"It's Gordon."

Damn. She said neutrally, "Yes?"

"Is that really you? You sound all muffled."

She took off the filter mask and said crisply, "What is it, Gordon?"

He was direct, one of the things she'd liked about him, when she still liked things about him. "There was no kidnapping Thursday at Hingham."

That threw her. "Are you sure? Could there possibly be a child missing but the parents didn't report it, or...or maybe just another burglary, the algorithms used those to—"

"I know my damn job. If there were so much as a misplaced *screwdriver* in this town tonight, we'd fucking well know about it."

In his unaccustomed irritability she heard his tension over the situation. Unless his tension was over her, which she definitely did not want.

She said, "I explained to you that the burglaries complicated the algorithms, made them more than a simple linear progression. It was a judgment call which ones to include. I might have included some that were inside jobs with no forced entry, I might have missed some that—"

"I know all that. You did explain it. Several times. But the fact is that your predictive program isn't working, and you need to fix it in part because I've staked my credibility with the A-Dic on it."

Not like him to say so much. Her temper rose. "You can't blame this failure on me, Gordon. I told you when you approached me at the university that predictive algorithms with this kind of data—"

"I know what you told me. Stop talking to me like I'm an idiot. Just put this new non-data in and give me something else I can work with. If you really can."

"I'll do what is possible," she said stiffly.

"Great. Call me whenever it's done." He hung up, everything else unsaid between them.

Julie closed the door to the freezing nursery-to-be, put on a heavy sweater, and went to her computer.

APRIL 2014

FROM THE FLOOR of the Atlantic Ocean rose the longest mountain range in the world, separating huge tectonic plates. All at once a northern section of the African Plate moved closer to the South American Plate. The move was only an inch, and the resulting earthquake so slight it was felt by nobody. But the hydrophones set around the ocean picked up the shift from its low-frequency sonic rumbles, sending the information to monitoring stations on four continents.

"¡Mirar esto!" a technician called to his superior in Spain.

"Regardez!"

"Ei, olhar para esta!"

"Kijk naar dit!"

"Will you fucking take a look at that!"

2035

Kara started screaming as soon as Pete came through the archway to the children's room.

Thirteen children played or slept or learned in this large open space. Like all interior Shell rooms, it had featureless white metal walls, floor, and ceiling. There was no visible lighting but the room was suffused with a glow that brightened at "day" and dimmed at "night," although never to complete blackness. The Shell contained only those objects originally gathered by Tesslies before they destroyed the world, or else objects seized on Grabs with the machinery the aliens had supplied a year ago. Pallets of blankets either thin and holey or else thick and new. Pillows on the floor for the adults to sit on. Many bright plastic toys, from the time that one of Jenna's Grabs had landed her in something called a "Wal-Mart." That Grab was famous. Jenna, almost as smart as her mother, had used her ten minutes to lash together three huge shopping carts and frantically fill them with everything in the closest aisles, toys and tools and clothing and "soft goods." The pillows had come from that Grab, and the sheets and blankets that made both bedding and clothes for those who didn't happen at the moment to fit into any clothes Grabbed at other stores. The shopping carts were now used to trundle things along the central corridor.

One wall held McAllister's calendar. Crayons and paint just slid off the metal walls, but McAllister had put up a large sheet with packing tape and on that she kept careful track of how long humanity had been in the Shell. As a little boy Pete had sat in front of that calendar in a learning circle and learned to count. He'd been taught to read, too, although until Jenna's Grab all the letters had to be written on a blanket using burned twigs from the farm. Now the Shell had six precious books, which everyone read over and over. All the pages were smeary and torn at the edges.

The children's room—and many other rooms as well—held piles of buckets. These had been here from the beginning; evidently the Tesslies considered buckets important. The Shell contained whole rooms full of buckets, from fist-sized (these were used as bowls and cups) to big ones on the farm. The buckets could be stuck to each other with something in tubes that Jenna had brought back from her Wal-Mart Grab. A shoulder-high wall of stuck-together buckets divided the babies' corner from the rest of the children's room. And, of course, the buckets were used for pissing and shitting.

Jenna would never do another Grab. Her deformities were worse than most, and now her spine would not hold up her body for more than a few minutes of painful movement. It wouldn't be long before one of the shopping carts would have to trundle her. But despite the constant pain, she retained the sweet nature she had inherited from McAllister, and now she sat on a pillow, back against the wall beside the open door, reading to four kids sprawled on the floor. *Goodnight Moon*. Pete knew it well.

Kara looked up, saw Pete, and shrieked. "No! No! Nooooooo!" The child threw herself on the floor and kicked her bare feet against the metal.

McAllister picked her up. "No, sweetheart, no... ssshhhhhhh, Kara-love, ssshhhhh...."

Kara went on screaming until Caity rushed over, took Kara from McAllister, and carried her away, tossing a reproachful glance over her shoulder at Pete. He'd never liked Caity, not even when they were kids themselves. *"She's too much like you,"* McAllister had said to him once, and Pete had hid from McAllister in the far end of the Shell for an entire day. He still didn't like Caity, not even when he was having sex with her.

Jenna said, "How are you, Pete?"

"Great, just great, on this great ol' day in the morning." Almost immediately he regretted saying that. Jenna loved the songs Bridget had crooned to them as kids, and she'd loved Bridget. At Bridget's funeral a few months ago, Jenna had sobbed and sobbed.

Jenna didn't react to the sarcasm. She, of all the Six, was the best at setting aside her own feelings for the common good. Terrell and Paolo were pretty good at it, too. Pete, Ravi, and Caity often failed.

Failed, failed, failed... That was Pete's song, unless he made hatred sing louder.

Jenna said, "I'm glad you recovered from your Grab. Kara is coming along very well—"

"Unless she sees me, of course."

"—and Petra is a darling."

"I better go Outside to give Kara a chance to adjust."

McAllister said, sharply for her, "That's enough of that talk, Pete. Come with me."

As if anyone could really get Outside!

But he followed her meekly, wishing for the hundred hundredth time that he had Jenna's patience. Ravi's physical strength and good looks. Anything that anyone else had and he didn't. Wishing he could seize McAllister's waist and take her into one of the rooms at the far end of the Shell, just the two of them and a blanket... His cock rose.

Not a good time! Still, he was glad he was only infertile, not impotent like Paolo. *"Pre-embryonic genetic damage is a capricious thing,"* McAllister had said. *"We were lucky you Six survived at all."*

Lucky. Great, just great, on this great ol' day in the morning.

McAllister led Pete around the bucket-wall to the babies' corner. Three infants lay asleep on blankets, watched over by Ravi, who didn't much like babies but it was his turn for this duty. Ravi was the least deformed of the Six. His eyes were permanently crossed, but his body was strong and, even though he was a year younger than Pete, he was taller and heavier. With thick dark hair and a handsome face, he looked the most like the princes in *The Illustrated Book of Fairy Tales*. Sometimes Pete hated him for that, although in general they got along well enough. Ravi was his biological half-brother, after all. Not that that counted for much; what counted was the good of all.

"Look," McAllister said to Pete, "at the treasure you brought us."

Petra lay asleep on a blanket, a square of plastic between it and the clumsy diaper made of another blanket. On top she wore a very faded yellow shirt too big for her. Her tiny pink mouth, the little curled fists with the creases at the wrists, the shape of her head... She was a perfect human person and of course she would be fertile. Radiation levels had subsided enough by now, McAllister had said, although Pete didn't really understand what that meant. It didn't matter. What mattered was that he had done this thing: brought back a perfect, precious boost to the restarting of humanity on Earth. Someday that restarting would move Outside, McAllister said.

If the Tesslies permitted it.

McAllister put her thin hands on either side of Pete's face and turned him toward her. "Listen to me, dear heart. I am making you this baby's father. You are now responsible for her life and, as much as possible, her happiness. Do you understand me? I put Petra's life in your hands. You are her father."

Both Pete and Ravi gaped at her. No one in the

Shell was "father" or "mother" to any kid taken on a Grab! Everyone was responsible for the good of all, always. Why now, why Petra, why Pete? The questions were lost in the feel of McAllister's hands on his face.

"Why him?" Ravi blurted. "Is it because he's the oldest?"

McAllister didn't answer. She never answered anything she didn't choose to. But she gave Ravi a look that Pete couldn't read, and didn't want to. All he wanted was for her to keep on holding his face between her long slim fingers, forever and ever.

She didn't. But he could feel her hands long after she took them away, could feel his own deep blush, could feel the burden, welcome because she had given it, that McAllister had just placed on his heart. To turn his red face away from her, he gazed down at Petra.

"Hey," he said to the baby, who woke and immediately shit her diaper.

NOVEMBER 2013

JULIE SAT IN HER APARTMENT, studying the graphs on her computer screen. Her desk was jammed against the living room window. Beyond the glass a few flakes of early snow drifted through darkness. Cars swooshed through street slush and swept ghostly patterns of light across the ceiling.

The kidnappings and mysterious store burglaries had followed an erratic path, but the rough outline was clear. The first abduction—the first they knew about and had included in the data, she corrected herself—had been in Sarasota a year ago. October 16 2011: Tommy Candless, age six. Parents divorced, and the child basically a Ping-Pong ball for power struggles between them. John Candless, who did not have custody, had grabbed his son and run before, but he'd easily been caught by state troopers since he hadn't even had the sense to leave Florida. Heather Candless had one conviction for DWI. Julie wasn't even positive that Tommy wasn't squirreled away with some obscure relative or friend somewhere that Gordon's task force had failed to discover. Or the child could have been killed and the body never found. Both parents seemed to her capable of even that in their intense hatred for each other.

Drop Tommy from the data? Would that help? No, her gut said to leave him in. She did.

The path of subsequent abductions moved roughly up the East Coast, sometimes swerving inland, sometimes back-tracking. The intervals weren't even, coming in clusters that themselves weren't even. Nine children after Tommy, including Kara and Jennifer Carter. The kids ranged from ten months old to Tommy's six years. Seven girls, three boys. Two hysterical witnesses, one relatively calm one (but her baby hadn't been taken; she'd fought off the young abductress). One hysterical witness had been pushed over the slippery edge of her already advancing illness into an institutional schizophrenia, which did not help the FBI Assistant Director to trust her credibility.

The big problem with the data, as Julie had told Gordon, were the store burglaries. Here, too, the MO was the same: no forced entry, no money taken, seemingly random grabs of diverse merchandise, including shopping carts. Why take shopping carts, both worthless and conspicuous? Why take an entire display of Reese's Peanut Butter Cups? At Wal-Mart's, why take pillows and leave untouched a display of diamond rings? And should the Baltimore Kohl's burglary be included or not? How about that earlier one in Georgia? Or the one in the New Jersey convenience store? That store had had a broken back window, which might have taken it off the list of no-forced-entry burglaries. However, a neighbor walking his dog at 3:00 a.m. thought he heard glass breaking. He shouted and saw kids run away, empty-handed, so did that mean there were two incidents at the same store at the same night, a coincidence?

She played with the data, putting in one incident, taking out another, changing the patterns. The maddening thing was that the patterns were there, and not just in MOs. The numbers showed patterns, too: nonlinear, closer to fractals than to conventional graphs, but nonetheless there. And the numbers should have pointed to another abduction or burglary in Hingham, Massachusetts, on Thursday. Which hadn't happened. So obviously she had included something erroneous, or left something out, or missed something altogether.

She sat far into the night, scrutinizing data.

APRIL 2014

IN XINJIANG AUTONOMOUS REGION of northern China, the cotton fields lay serene under the sun. Acre upon acre of the plants stretched to the horizon, dark green leaves a little dusty from lack of rain. Clouds overhead, however, promised water soon. The white boles had only just begun to open, filling the green fields with lopsided polka dots. A golden eagle coasted on an air current, a darker speck against the gray clouds. To the south lay the ancient Silk Road, and much farther south, the majestic and forbidding peaks of the Kunlun Mountains.

On the roots of the cotton plants, bacteria mutated.

2035

THE GRAB MACHINERY was Tesslie, of course. It sat in its own room in the Shell, a room without a door just down the central corridor from the farm and the children's room. Someone had to sit there day and night because no one knew when the machinery would brighten. When it did, they had only a few minutes to get someone on it. Then ten minutes in Before to make a Grab. The whole system was stupid. Pete said so to McAllister, often.

"It isn't our machinery, remember," she said. "We don't know how the Tesslies manage time, or intervals of time. We don't know how they think."

"They think it's fun to destroy the Earth, rescue a few Survivors, put them in the Shell, and watch them for twenty years."

"There's no reason to think they watch us."

"There's no reason to think they don't."

"They need machinery, Pete—they're aliens but not gods. I see no cameras here."

Pete turned away because McAllister had just, as she so often did, gone abruptly beyond him. He didn't know what "gods" were, although some of the

Survivors had babbled about them when Pete was little, and Darlene still did. She sang songs about green pastures and washing in blood and rowing boats ashore, all in her scratchy tuneless very loud voice. However, nobody listened to Darlene, who was a nasty old woman. Pete wasn't too sure about the word "camera" either, although it seemed to be a non-Tesslie machinery that made pictures. Pete didn't know how machines could draw that fast. But how could the Grab do what it did?

The machinery sat in the center of the room, looking like nothing but a gray metal platform a few inches above the floor. If he climbed onto it, ordinarily nothing happened. But sometimes the platform started to glow and then it became a stupid invisible door. No, not a door. Something else. Whatever it was, if you jumped on the platform and went through it, you had ten minutes in Before.

The Grabs usually came a few close together, then long weeks of no brightening. After the Grab when Pete got Kara and Petra, while he'd been feverish with his infected foot, Paolo had fallen asleep and missed the whole thing. Even if Paolo hadn't been sick, Pete couldn't really blame him. Watching the Grab machine do nothing, with only your own thoughts to occupy you, was easily the most boring duty on the roster.

But did the Tesslies watch humanity? That was the question that now consumed Pete. Did they watch Pete and Caity when they had sex? Even though Pete didn't like Caity, she was his only choice. Jenna had grown too fragile, and the kids from the Grab were still too young. That was why they were Grabbed, of course—to have sex when they were older. The girls would be fertile. The boys would be fertile, too, but the Shell needed a lot more girls than boys. None of the Six apparently were fertile, and the four Survivors left were too old to have babies.

But they had had a lot of sex when they were young and newly in the Shell. Even way back then they had been trying to start humanity all over again. Lots of sex—Pete got hard just imagining it—and lots of babies, most of which died.

But had the fucking bastards (more of Darlene's useful words) watched while the Survivors had all that sex? Did they watch Pete and Caity? And what was a "bastard," anyway?

Pete tried to sneak across the corridor from the farm to the children's room. It had been his turn for fertilizer duty, a job he hated. The fertilizer was made from everybody's shit. You dumped it into a huge closed metal box (more Tesslie machinery!) and the box did something to it. When it fell out a hole into a bucket, it didn't smell like shit anymore and McAllister said it couldn't make you sick. But it still *looked* like shit. Pete had been collecting shit buckets from all over the Shell, trundling them along the wide central corridor on a shopping cart and dumping them into the fertilizer box. Then he had to rinse each bucket thoroughly under the disinfectant waterfall, which was a continuous rain of blue water that shot out of a wall and disappeared into a hole in the floor. Just after he'd rinsed the last bucket, the fertilizer machine delivered a load of fertilizer. Pete tried to pretend he hadn't seen the bucket fill, so that spreading the fertilizer would have to be the next person's job, but Darlene caught him.

"Ha! Don't be sneaking off before the job's done! I seen you!"

"I wasn't sneaking off!"

"Sure you was. You're bone lazy, Pete. A wild one for sure. Go spread that bucket."

When Bridget died, Pete wished it had been Darlene instead. "Where should I spread this?" He picked up the bucket of fertilizer. "On the soy?"

"Them ain't soy," she said scathingly. "Them are some concoction the Tesslies dreamed up and don't you think nothing different, boy! Them plants will probably poison us yet!"

"Yeah, right," Pete said. Darlene was crazy. The Tesslies keeping humans alive for twenty years, giving them Grab machinery to get fertile kids to make more humans, just to poison the whole lot.

Then he realized that Darlene's craziness was driving him to defend the Tesslies, and he threw the brown gunk—it still looked like shit!—harder than necessary onto the soy. Or whatever it was. "High-protein, dense-calorie plants," Jenna had told him once. McAllister was teaching Jenna and Paolo all the science she knew from Before, so it wouldn't be lost. The other Survivors had done the same, but they hadn't known nearly as much. "We must save everything we can," she always said.

Pete spread the fertilizer through the soy. There was enough for half the onion bed, too. Then he rinsed the bucket. Darlene watched him every minute.

Darlene was in charge of the farm. In a way that was weird because Eduardo was the Survivor who had been studying plants when the Tesslies put him into the Shell. "Ecobiology," McAllister had called it. But that just meant that the plants Eduardo knew about were wild ones, and he told Pete that no special knowledge was needed to grow the vegetables on the farm. Besides, nobody wanted Darlene anywhere near the Grab children. She was too mean.

The farm was the biggest room in the Shell, with rows and rows of raised beds holding various crops, crossed by long metal pipes that leaked water. The farm also housed the disinfecting waterfall and the clean-water waterfall, from which endless buckets of water were hauled for drinking, washing, cooking. Here, too, stood the raised section of the floor that could be turned hot by pressing a button. Bridget had been especially good at simmering vegetable stews on the hot box, in buckets. Now Eduardo did it, less well. The farm smelled good, of dirt and water and cooking, and it would have been a lovely place if it hadn't been for Darlene.

"'Rock of ages,'" she sang in her tuneless, scratchy voice while Pete spread fertilizer. "'Cleft for me'... You spread that even, Pete, you hear me? Bone lazy!" He escaped as soon as he could and went to see Petra.

She was awake, lying on a blanket, kicking her fat little legs. Caity was on duty in the babies' corner behind its wall of buckets. At the sight of her, Pete again thought of sex, but Caity didn't seem interested, and after a moment he realized that he wasn't, either. Not with Caity.

She said, "Did you hear about Xiaobo?"

"What about him?

"He's dying."

It took Pete a moment to take it in, even though the news wasn't unexpected. "Where?"

"His room."

McAllister would be there. Pete walked back through the children's room. At the sight of him, Kara started screaming. How long was *that* going to keep on? Kara would just have to get over it. The older children, three to five years old, were clustered around Jenna in a learning circle, being taught to count buckets and read letters and sing songs. When they were older, McAllister and Eduardo would teach them about stars and atoms and the digestive system. *"We must save everything we can."*

McAllister wasn't with Xiaobo, but Eduardo and Paolo were.

Eduardo was the oldest of the Survivors, and looked it. Only a few years older than McAllister, he seemed to Pete to be older than time. Thinning gray hair straggled around a deeply lined face. Eduardo, a quiet and courteous man, had never lost his soft Spanish accent, and when Pete had been little, he'd loved to have Eduardo tell him stories. He was Paolo's father, and the two looked alike, although even now Eduardo was stronger than the sickly Paolo. The two sat one on each side of Xiaobo, who lay on a pile of blankets in the bare little room. Paolo held Xiaobo's hand. Next to these three, Pete actually felt strong and whole.

He knelt at the foot of the nest of blankets. "Xiaobo."

The dying man opened his eyes. When Pete had been very small, Xiaobo's eyes had fascinated him: small, slanted, hooded by a fold of skin. At the same time, Xiaobo had scared him because he spoke so weird. English had come slowly to him, and now that Pete was grown himself he realized how lonely Xiaobo must have been in the Shell, the only Survivor of his people, the only one who could not talk to anyone else.

"Xiaobo, are you hurting?"

"No."

"Can I get you anything?"

"Nothing. I go now, Pete."

"You don't know that you—"

"It is time. I go." He closed his eyes again, and smiled.

I will never go that quietly. The thought built itself in his mind, solid as the Shell itself. *I will not*.

He didn't know what else to say, but then there wasn't time to say anything else. Tommy, at seven, the oldest of the children and the only one yet permitted to leave the children's room alone, raced into Xiaobo's room. "The Grab is bright!"

Pete leapt up. "Where's McAllister?"

"I don't know!" The boy throbbed with excitement.

Unlike Kara, Tommy was one who'd adapted easily to his new life.

"It's Ravi's turn to go on the Grab," Pete said. "Where's Ravi?"

"I don't know that either! Anyway Terrell was supposed to go because McAllister said he's twelve now but Terrell got sick again and threw up and Darlene came over from the farm and told him to go lie down in his room like a useless stone."

Darlene wasn't supposed to tell Grab watchers anything. Pete, Paolo, and Eduardo looked at each other. How much longer would the platform stay bright? Paolo said, "You just went, Pete. Caity can go."

"She's on baby duty," Pete said. And he was off running down the corridor, cursing Ravi for being—where? Doing what? It was Ravi's turn, not Terrell's! And why had McAllister changed the duty roster?

Tommy raced at his heels. "Can I go, Pete? Can I, huh? Can I go, too?"

"No!"

The boy stopped cold and shouted after him, "You're selfish! You're a selfish piggy who doesn't care about the good of all! I'm telling! I am!"

Pete reached the Grab machinery and climbed onto the platform.

DECEMBER 2013

JULIE SAT ON HER NEW sleep sofa in her living room, which had grown smaller with the addition of her desk, smaller still with the broad sofa, and yet again smaller with the Christmas tree crowded into a corner. The scent of Douglas fir drifted through the room. She was wrapping presents in bright metallic paper. Jake was flying in from Wyoming and although they weren't particularly close, each was the only family the other had since their parents had died in a plane crash three years ago, and it *was* Christmas. For Christmas you gathered family, even if half your heritage was Jewish. Jake, who would sleep on the extended sofa with his feet against the tree, was about to discover that he had one more family member than he thought.

She hadn't told him earlier about her pregnancy because he was going to disapprove. Not of her getting pregnant, although he would undoubtedly consider that careless, but of her having and keeping the baby. Jake, deeply ambitious, had risen rapidly through the ranks of the U.S. Geological Survey. He was proud of both her career and his own, and he would frown at the year-long sabbatical she was taking to even have the baby, let alone the professional sacrifices that she knew perfectly well would follow. Julie did not intend to have her child raised by a succession of nannies, Even if she had had room for a nanny. She would make the transition from brilliant professor to brilliant consultant and work at home, perhaps teaching one course per semester as a sideline. Already she had feelers out for potential projects with various industries and government agencies.

She taped wrapping paper around a Bunny Mine, the current hot toy for toddlers. Her daughter, now a four-and-a-half-month fetus, wouldn't be playing with a Bunny Mine for at least a year, but it would look cute on the shelves that Julie had put up in the nursery. The nursery was finished. The layette was complete. The childbirth classes began in January. It was all planned out, everything under control.

Julie had just begun to wrap a sweater for Jake when her cell rang. "Hello, Julie Kahn speaking."

"This is Gordon."

Her lips pursed. She hadn't heard from him in nearly a month, since she'd given him her best stab at the revised data on the kidnappings. Since then she'd watched the Massachusetts, Connecticut, Rhode Island, and Maine newspapers; no child had been reported as missing. Plenty of burglaries, of course— theft always picked up as Christmas approached— but without Gordon's input, Julie had no way of knowing which ones fit the MO that the task force had been pursuing.

"Hello, Gordon," she said neutrally, hoping this call wasn't personal.

It wasn't. He said, "I wanted you to know that the A-Dic pulled the plug on the task force. Each kidnapping has been assigned to a local Special Agent in Charge. The A-Dic just doesn't believe a connective enterprise exists."

"The mathematical pattern exists."

"Maybe. No more kidnappings since Kara and Jennifer Carter. No store burglaries with that MO, either."

"Before this there have been long stretches between incidents."

He made a noise she recognized: the verbal equivalent of a shrug. Gordon was moving on. He was not a man to hold on to what he could not control.

She said, "The pattern exists, Gordon."

Instead of agreeing or arguing, he said, "How are you?"

"Still pregnant, if that's what you're asking."

"Can I come see you?"

"No. You're married, Gordon."

"There were two of us in those motel rooms, Julie."

"I'm not accusing you of anything. I take complete responsibility for my actions, and for this result. It doesn't involve you."

"Damn it, I'm the father!"

She drew a deep breath. "Only biologically. I don't mean that to be nasty, Gordon. You have no room for us in your life, and anyway I don't want that. I don't think you do, either, not really. Please just leave me be."

"If you need money—"

"I don't. Bye, Gordon. I'm sorry about the task force, because I still think there's something there."

"But Julie—"

Gently she pressed the disconnect button on her cell.

Within her body, the baby moved, and she put her hand on her belly and watched the lights twinkle on and off on the little Christmas tree above the festive packages.

2035

IT WASN'T DARK, and it wasn't light. It wasn't anything. *I'm dead*, Pete thought, as usual, but of course he wasn't, as usual.

When the nothing receded, disappointment warred with relief. There would be no little girls here. But there would be no fighting or dying, either. He stood in dim light inside a store filled with objects he couldn't even identify until he saw a big doll, life-size, with no head or arms or legs, wearing some of the objects. Oh—it was *clothing!* Skimpy filmy pants, strips of fancy cloth across the breasts, racks and racks of this stuff… All at once he pictured Caity wearing it, and then McAllister, and his cock rose and he groaned. He couldn't bring back stuff like this!

He glanced at his wrist to see how much time he had left, but of course he wasn't wearing the wrister. Terrell still had it. Now what?

He ran past the headless dolls wearing fancy skimpy things and discovered that around the corner were other parts of the store, that in fact it was as big as the children's room, maybe even bigger than the farm. The other areas held different stuff, as well as shopping carts. He grabbed one and started throwing things into it from under a sign labeled HOMEWARES. Blankets, towels, rugs—damn this was good!—and then pots and a big red tray and boxes of spoons and—

A dog came racing down a set of metal stairs, snarling and barking.

Pete screamed and climbed on top of the shopping cart, nearly slipping on the red tray and falling back off. The dog leaped and its teeth closed on Pete's leg, although only for a moment before the animal's weight sent it crashing back to the floor. Pete screamed, grabbed the tray, and held it in front of him. With his other hand he yanked a pot free of the stuff in the shopping cart and threw it at the dog, missing it. How much time was left—*how much?* Blood streamed down his leg.

The dog leapt again, but it couldn't reach Pete on top of the cart. However, the impact of its body sent the cart skittering across the floor. Alarms sounded and lights came on. The dog barked and Pete shrieked at it.

The cart rolled past a display of DIGITAL FOTO FRAMES, heavy-looking metal squares. Pete grabbed one. Before he could throw it at the dog, the Grab took him back.

On the platform, the rolling shopping cart kept rolling. It crashed over the edge and tipped on its side. Pete fell heavily amid pots, rugs, blankets. For a moment his head rang, but nothing on him broke and he staggered up out of the debris, clutching the DIGITAL FOTO FRAME and more furious than he'd ever been in his life.

He roared at Tommy, "Where the fuck is Ravi?"

The child was not a weeper. He stared back, scared

but not budging, and said, "Where did you go?"

Others rushed into the Grab room: Darlene, Paolo, Eduardo. From down the corridor Caity and Jenna, who could not leave the children, screamed, "What is it? What is it?" But no Ravi, and no McAllister.

Pete pushed past everyone and ran down the corridor to the unused far end. Behind him Darlene cackled, "Oh, lovely, an electric fryer! Just what we need!"

Paolo, unable to keep up, called, "Wait, Pete! Wait!"

Tommy, easily able to keep up, ran beside him saying, "What is it? What, Pete? What?"

He found them in the maze of rooms near the tip of the Shell. A blanket had been spread on the floor. McAllister had just slid her loose dress back onto her body, but Ravi was still naked, lying on the blanket, too drained and heavy to move. Pete recognized Ravi's sated heaviness; he'd felt it after sex with Caity. But never with McAllister: never, never, never.

She said, "Pete—"

"You fucking bastards."

Tommy gaped. "What is it? What?"

In rage and hurt and frustration, and before he knew he was going to do it, Pete threw the DIGITAL FOTO FRAME at McAllister. It grazed her on the side of the head and she cried out. Ravi leapt up and threw a punch at Pete. Pete dodged, Ravi missed, and Pete kicked him in the balls.

"Stop! That's enough!" McAllister shouted. But it wasn't her words, or even that she shouted—McAllister, who never raised her voice! It was the blood on her head, streaming down one cheek. *He had hurt McAllister*. He collapsed to the ground in tears.

Ravi was up and charging, but McAllister stopped him with a word. She bent over Pete. Now Paolo and Eduardo and Darlene were all there; Pete could see their bare feet from where he huddled on the floor. McAllister sent them all away with sharp commands, even Ravi, who snatched up his clothes as he left.

"Pete," she said, her voice soft again, "listen to me. Ravi—"

"You never would with me! You said it would cause trouble! You said for the good of all—"

"I know what I said. But listen to me, dear heart. Please listen, I know you're strong enough to listen. This *is* for the good of all. Ravi is fertile."

He stopped ranting, too desolate even for rage.

"You know I checked all of your sperm with the little microscope Jenna got on her Wal-Mart Grab. Ravi is the only one of you who is fertile. He's had sex with both Caity and Jenna, and neither got pregnant, and now Jenna is too fragile. This is the only chance left among ourselves."

"We have the Grab kids!"

"Yes, of course. But we need every soul we can get, you know that. The Tesslies could end the Grabs at any time. And we miss some of them."

"Well, Ravi just missed his. And so did Terrell because he was throwing up—did you know that? So I just did the Grab and nearly got killed!" He tried to wrench free of her, but McAllister held on and the truth was that he didn't want to get free.

He wanted what Ravi had had.

He put a hand on her breast. When she removed it, he forced her down onto the blanket.

"No, Pete," she said, calm as ever, "I know you wouldn't do that. That's not you. Dear heart, please try to understand. You have a deep, sweet nature and I know you *can* understand. For the good of all."

He let her up, gazing bleakly at the blood on her face. "I hurt you."

"And I hurt you. I'm deeply sorry for that, but we need to survive."

He said fiercely, "Did you like it?"

She touched his eyelids, one after the other, a delicate finger-kiss.

"Because Ravi liked it! I know!"

"I love you, Pete. I love you all."

He got to his feet and seized the DIGITAL FOTO FRAME. Something had to be his, something had to be outside of the "good of all," something had to be... He didn't know what his confused thoughts meant. But he said defiantly, stupidly, "I'm keeping this!"

"All right," McAllister said.

"It's mine! Just mine!" Nothing ever belonged to one person, nothing.

"All right," she repeated.

He clutched it, scowling at her, hating her, loving her. The silence stretched on. She waited, but he didn't know for what. For him to say something, for him to look away.

He looked away, down at the object in his hand, and said, "What is it?"

APRIL 2014

UNDER THE CANADIAN GLACIER, molten rock bubbled up from a fissure in the earth. When the pressure became great enough, the ground erupted. Lava met ice, which instantly boiled into steam. The magma hitting the steam exploded into miniscule fragments, sending pillar after pillar of ash billowing overhead. The magma was heavy on silica from the chamber it had breached earlier, which made it much more viscous and sticky than usual. That prevented air bubbles from escaping quickly and so pressure built relentlessly, leading to more and more explosions.

Ash blew southeast on a cold wind, toward Ontario and Quebec.

APRIL 2014

JULIE SAT in the Starbucks on K Street. Linda had just left, full of plans for her family, Julie, and the baby to take a cottage together in August on Maryland's Eastern Shore. "The baby'll be nearly four months by then, and it'll be such fun!" Julie wasn't sure about that—two weeks with Linda's noisy kids and noisier dogs? On the other hand, two weeks with Linda and Ted *would* be fun. Or two weeks in separate, side-by-side cottages. Or two weeks someplace else.

She frowned at the out-of-town newspaper she'd bought at World Wide News. The headlines were all about air traffic hopelessly snarled in Canada by blowing and drifting ash, but that was not what she stared at. *Was it or wasn't it?* Then, wryly: *I sound like a Clairol commercial.* And not even a current commercial. She was showing her age.

Again she read the short, not-very-informative article about the burglary in a small town in western Massachusetts, which was one of the projected paths of her original algorithm. A family-owned department store, one of the few left in the country, had been robbed of a collection of miscellaneous objects, primarily blankets, rugs, and cookware. Also a shopping cart, which was considered "an unusual theft for this kind of burglary." Julie wasn't sure what "kind of burglary" the small-town news stringer meant, but she knew what she was looking at. Shopping cart, no forced entry. This time, however, the store had had a guard dog, which had not been harmed. Drops of blood on the floor indicated that the "perpetrator" might have been harmed, but the police had as yet made no arrests.

Whose blood?

"May I sit here? There don't seem to be any free tables."

He was tall, attractive, dressed in a suit and tie. He carried the *Wall Street Journal*, folded to show the headline: FINANCIAL IMPACT OF COMING FRESH WATER SHORTAGES. Glancing at her ringless left hand, he smiled and sat down without waiting for an invitation. Julie stood, and as soon as the curve of her belly under her open coat came into view, his smile vanished.

Julie grinned. "Sure, the table's all yours."

Relief on that handsome face.

She buttoned her coat and waddled out. The OB had said she was gaining too much weight, once she'd stopped throwing up, but that otherwise everything was "progressing swimmingly," a phrase she had liked instantly. Little Alicia, swimming in her secret sea. The baby now had fully developed toenails. Her body could store calcium and phosphorus. She had begun to show the brain waves of REM sleep. What will you dream of, my darling?

Julie left Starbucks. Walking was supposed to be good for her, so she walked even though she had piles of work at home. Consulting work for a high-resolution space imagery firm, for a professor doing research on microbes, even for the Bureau, in a division different from Gordon's. Everybody, it seemed, needed well-recommended and high-priced mathematical insight. Things were working out well.

The air was crisp and cold, unusually cold for March. Julie walked briskly. Some kids who probably should have been in school ran frantically in the pocket park across the street, trying to get a kite aloft. Daffodils and tulips splotched the park with color.

Whose blood had been on the floor of that department store in western Massachusetts?

2035

THE DIGITAL FOTO FRAME held pictures that moved out of the frame so the next one could come in. Pete had never imagined anything like it. It was even better than the drawings in *The Illustrated Book of Fairy Tales* or *Goodnight Moon* because these pictures looked far more real. There were three, and Pete never tired of looking at them. He wouldn't let any others of the Six look at them, and for once McAllister did not insist that he share.

One of the pictures was of two children playing with a dog. This didn't look anything like the dog that had attacked Pete in the store. This dog was reddish and happy-looking, but Pete didn't like it anyway and sometimes he closed his eyes when that picture appeared. The other two were glorious. One was a beach like the place where he'd Grabbed Petra and Kara, but with mountains across the water, colored gold by a setting sun. The other showed a forest filled with trees and flowers. Pete had never seen mountains or sunset, but on Grabs he'd seen sunrise, several trees, and some flowers, and now it was wonderful to sit and gaze at them without the fear and tension of a Grab.

"Why aren't there more pictures?" he asked Eduardo. He was avoiding McAllister. It was a complaint, not a real question, but Eduardo had a real answer.

"There could be more if we had them to upload," he said in his soft accent. "These are just demonstration photos. You understand that the battery will run out eventually?"

"Of course," Pete said scornfully. Some of the children's toys from Jenna's famous Grab had used batteries, which all died.

"The more you use it, the less long it will last."

"I know." But he couldn't stop gazing at the DIGITAL FOTO FRAME.

He held it, clutched in one hand, during Xiaobo's funeral. The funeral room, located off the central corridor across from the Grab room, was yet another featureless white-metal room. There was absolutely nothing in it except the outline of the slot on the far wall, close to the floor, and the button set high on the opposite wall, by the door. Caity, Eduardo, Terrell, McAllister, Darlene, Ravi, and Pete attended the funeral. Also Tommy, now that he was nearly eight. Jenna and Paolo stayed with the Grab children.

It was Tommy's first funeral and he held tight to McAllister's hand, although to Pete he looked more interested than scared. Tommy was tough. Well, good. He'd have an easier time of it than some of the children. Kara still screamed every time she saw Pete.

Ravi, another tough one, stared down at Xiaobo's body, wrapped in their oldest blanket. On top of the body, as was the custom, lay one small thing that the dead person had cherished. For Xiaobo, it was a little stone statue of a fat smiling man that Xiaobo had had with him all the way back when the Tesslies put him in the Shell. Bridget had gone with a lock of hair from a baby of hers that had been stillborn.

Ravi's face remained blank. Caity and Terrell leaned against the wall, tearful. Darlene, Eduardo, and McAllister, the last of the Survivors, had so many feelings on their faces that Pete could barely look at them.

His own feelings troubled him, because there didn't seem to be enough of them. He'd known Xiaobo his whole life, had worked beside him, eaten with him, probably been diapered by him when Pete was a baby. They hadn't talked much, given Xiaobo's limited English, but he'd always been kind to Pete, to everyone. Right up until this last illness, Xiaobo had been a hard worker. And all Pete felt was that he should feel more, along with a vague curiosity about what it felt like to be dead. Darlene said that the ghosts of billions murdered by the Tesslies haunted the Shell. But Pete had never seen a ghost at all, and anyway where in the Shell could you fit billions of them? He wasn't exactly sure how much a "billion" was, but it sounded large.

Eduardo said in his musical voice, "As for man, his days are like grass. As a flower of the field, so he flourishes. For the wind passes over it, and it is gone, and its place remembers it no more." That was what he always said at funerals, and Pete always hated it. It sounded sad, and anyway it was stupid. Xiaobo wasn't grass—people were made of skin and bones and blood. There was no wind inside the Shell. And this place certainly would remember Xiaobo. Pete would, and so would the other Six and Darlene and Eduardo and, of course, McAllister.

Her words made more sense. "To the Earth we commit the body of our friend and family, Lung Xiaobo. His bones and tissues and heart will enrich the land and help to make it one to which humanity will, someday, return. Go with our gratitude, Xiaobo, and our love."

Darlene began to sing, another of her awful scratchy songs with words Pete didn't understand. There were so many things he didn't understand, starting with how McAllister could bear to have sex with Ravi. He hated him, he hated her, he hated everything. He clutched his DIGITAL FOTO FRAME tighter.

Darlene howled, "'Abide with me, 'tis eventide…'"

When the song was finished, McAllister pressed the funeral button. A section of the wall opened, a slot near the floor three feet wide and two high. Xiaobo didn't need that much room. Some unseen force pulled him into the wall. Tommy squatted to peer inside, just as Pete had done when he was little. Now, after being present at three funerals for Survivors and six for miscarriages, Pete knew there was nothing to see. The slot opened into a small bare featureless space, and the other side wouldn't open to deposit Xiaobo's body Outside until the first wall closed up.

Darlene bawled another song, this one about the

land being beautiful with spacious skies and a lot of grain, but Pete wasn't listening. He watched Ravi, who had turned his gaze to McAllister. Ravi looked the way he used to when there was a treat Grabbed from a store—oh, those Reese's Peanut Butter Cups!—and Ravi had tried to figure a way to get a bite of another child's share. Pete's hand tightened on the DIGITAL FOTO FRAME. He wanted to throw it at Ravi, to get his hands around Ravi's neck and squeeze... No, he didn't. Ravi was his half-brother. Yes, he did—Ravi had sex with McAllister, he was going to have more sex with McAllister, Pete wanted to kill him—

Ravi caught Pete's look and glared back.

The funeral was over. People moved away, returning to their duties. Caity stomped off, covering whatever softer feelings she had with vague bad temper. Pete lingered, and Tommy stayed with him. When they were the only two left in the funeral room, Tommy demanded, "How does McAllister know that the fucking bastard Tesslies will really put Xiaobo's body Outside to help grass to come back?"

Tommy must have been listening to Darlene. "McAllister knows."

"But how?"

Pete looked down at the intense little face. "Well, you didn't see any other bodies in there, did you? We've had a lot of funerals—you know that from learning circles. If the bodies weren't dumped out, they would just pile up in there."

Tommy considered. "Maybe the Tesslies just put

them in a fertilizer machine. Like shit. And then we spread them on the farm."

Pete had never thought of this. He could see that Tommy wished he hadn't thought of it, either. He knelt beside Tommy and said firmly, "No, that doesn't happen. The Tesslies told McAllister."

"I thought she never talked to them."

"Well, then they got her to understand some other way, like they got her to understand to press the funeral button, and how the fertilizer machine works and the Grab machinery and everything else." Actually, Pete wasn't sure how any of that had happened. Maybe the Survivors just figured everything out by themselves.

"All right," Tommy said. "But why do we believe the Tesslies?"

A good question. But not one that Pete wanted troubling Tommy. "We believe McAllister. You know how smart she is, right?"

"Yeah."

"Then there you have it, laddie." One of Bridget's favorite expressions.

"Okay." And then, "But I have another question."

"Go ahead."

"Why are you and Ravi mad at each other?"

Pete stood. This he was not going to discuss with Tommy.

"It's because Ravi had sex with McAllister, right? But you have sex with Caity. And when he wasn't sick, Terrell tried to have sex with Jenna, only she said he was still too young. And—"

Was there anything the kid didn't know? Pete said, "I want privacy on this." Those were words they all learned young, and learned to respect. *A necessity in such a small, closed family*, McAllister often said.

Tommy said, "Can I see the DIGITAL FOTO FRAME? Please, Pete, please please please?"

"All right." He turned it on, let the pictures move through the frame once each. Tommy watched, rapt. He reached out one finger to touch the mountain range. When Pete turned off the DIGITAL FOTO FRAME, Tommy sighed the same way he did right after Jenna finished reading aloud a fairy tale.

"Now go back to the children's room," Pete said.

Tommy said importantly, "I have *farm duty*."

"Oh. Then go do that."

Tommy left the funeral room, said, "Oh, hi," to someone in the corridor, and ran off. Pete tensed. If that was Ravi out there, waiting for him…

It was McAllister. "Pete, I want to talk with you."

"I want privacy on this," Pete said, with as much coldness as he could.

She smiled. "You don't even know what 'this' is yet, so how can you want privacy on it?"

He gazed sullenly at the wall behind her.

"What I wanted to say was thank you for being so good with Tommy. He's more unsure inside than he shows. Jenna says sometimes in bed he still cries for his mother. But he adores you and looks up to you, and you're such a good influence on him."

Pete glared at her. "I know what you're doing. You're trying to make me feel good so I won't fight

Ravi. Well, he's the one who wants to fight me. Didn't you see him smirk at me during the funeral?"

"I saw you smirking and glaring at each other. That has to stop. Pete, there is a statement from Before, said by a very smart and wise man, that the biggest threat to any society is its own young males between the ages of fourteen and twenty-four. Do you understand what that means?"

"No."

"It means—"

"I want privacy on this," Pete said and walked away. Whether or not the words fit—who the fuck cared, anyway?

APRIL 2014

IN THE COMPLEX network of faults in the Pacific Seismic Network, a thrust fault two hundred miles off the shore of Japan abruptly moved, as had happened before. The seabed deformed, vertically displacing an enormous volume of water. A huge wave rose on the ocean, long and low enough that an oil tanker barely noticed when it passed beneath its hull. As the wave raced toward shore, the shallower water both slowed and raised it. By the time the tsunami broke on Tokyo, the highest wave crested at ninety-four feet of water, smashing and inundating the city as well as the country far inland.

This had been predicted for a long time as a possibility for Tokyo. Only a few years earlier, it had happened south of that ancient city, with devastating results. Not the prediction, not the unfairness of being struck twice within a few years, not Japan's excellent tsunami-warning system—none of it lessened the horrific destruction.

2035

PETE SAT CROSS-LEGGED in his secret room by the Shell wall, gazing out. The room wasn't all that secret anymore; McAllister knew where it was, and Tommy had followed him here. Since Xiaobo's funeral, Pete had had unhappy sex with Caity here. Twice. The second time she'd bitten his ear; she was always rougher than he was. He wasn't going to do it with her anymore. He'd just masturbate.

The DIGITAL FOTO FRAME was in his hand, but Pete wasn't looking at it. He was looking at a miracle.

Crouched against the clear impenetrable wall, head wobbling as he craned his neck as far left as it would go, Pete saw a flash of green. *A piece of grass*. Several blades of grass, or something like grass, pushed out of the ground. "Volcanic rock," McAllister had once called it: "I think we're on the collapsed lip of a caldera." Pete didn't know what that meant, but he knew what the grasses meant.

The Earth was coming back. And he was the first to see it.

He didn't want to tell anyone. Or rather he did, he wanted to speak the incredible words out loud, but he also didn't want anyone else to know the secret.

Maybe Darlene was right: he was "a wild one." But that's what he wanted. He crept from the room, through the maze of tiny rooms at this end of the Shell, and along the corridor to the children's room.

It was so early that the kids lay asleep on blankets, some in diapers and some in little clothes that happened to fit at the moment. Karim, who didn't like clothes, slept naked, clutching a stuffed toy. The non-walking babies lay behind their bucket wall, with Jenna on duty. She was asleep, too. Pete knelt beside Petra and scooped her up with his good arm.

Petra didn't wake. Pete started around the bucket wall, then turned back. He didn't want to worry Jenna if she woke and found Petra gone. So he laid the DIGITAL FOTO FRAME on Petra's nest of blankets.

In the larger area, Tommy woke. Instantly he was on his feet, rubbing his eyes with his knuckles. His hair stood up in all directions. "Where are you going? Can I come, too?"

"SSShhhh! No. You stay here."

The boy's face, still puffy with sleep, went sad. Pete whispered, "You stay here now, Tommy, and later I'll take you on a big adventure."

"Really? What?"

Pete had no idea. But he couldn't think of anything else to deter Tommy. So he just shook his head and repeated, "You'll see. Stay here."

Tommy stayed. Pete carried Petra, who grew heavier with each step, to the secret room. She woke when he put her on the floor by the window.

"See, Petra—see the grass? The Earth is coming back!"

The baby screwed up her face and whimpered.

Ridiculously disappointed, Pete gazed alone at the grasses, jiggling Petra to quiet her. This didn't work. She whimpered louder, wailed a few times, and worked herself up to full, hungry screaming. Why were babies so much trouble? There should be a better way to restart humanity!

Since there wasn't, Pete crossly scooped up Petra to return her to Jenna, who would probably want him to stay to help with the children. At least he could get his DIGITAL FOTO FRAME back. He could trust Jenna not to touch it, but maybe not Tommy.

He had just left the maze, carrying the wailing Petra, when Tommy ran toward him. "Pete, you gotta come—McAllister's sick!"

His blood froze. McAllister. One by one the Survivors had sickened and died—"badly weakened immune systems, slow-growing cancers, and a fresh influx of microorganisms with each Grab," McAllister had said, but only Paolo and Jenna understood the words. If it was now McAllister's turn... They could not do without McAllister.

"She's in the farm," Tommy said. He added, "You didn't say I couldn't go there, only that I couldn't follow you!"

Pete didn't care where Tommy went. He put Petra down in the middle of the corridor and ran.

She was beside the fertilizer machine, puking into a bucket. There shouldn't have been a bucket there, unless one was being rinsed out in the disinfectant stream. McAllister must have brought a shit bucket with her and rinsed it out, but why? Today Caity was on shit-bucket duty. McAllister straightened and raised the hem of her loose homemade dress to wipe her mouth. She saw Tommy and Pete staring at her.

Tommy blurted, "Are you going to die? Like Bridget and Xiaobo?"

"No," McAllister said. She closed her eyes briefly.

"Then why are you—"

"Tommy, go to the children's room. Now."

All the children obeyed McAllister, without bribes or arguments. Tommy went, although he muttered and scowled. Pete said nothing. But when she'd raised her dress he had seen, and she knew it. As the oldest of the Six he'd seen enough bellies curved like that: Bridget's, Sarah's, Jessica's, Hannah's. But not for a long, long time.

"Pete—"

"You're pregnant."

"Yes."

"From sex with Ravi."

McAllister didn't answer; no need.

Pete said the first ugly thing that popped up from his foul-tasting hatred. "It'll die. Like all the other babies."

Something painful passed behind McAllister's eyes, but she said only, "Maybe not. You Six survived, including my Jenna. Pete, you are going to have to come to grips with this. It's reality, and not only that, it's a joyful reality for the good of all. Every additional soul expands our gene pool, gives us one more chance to restart humanity. You know that, and you're no longer a child. You must accept this. If you can, be happy for all of us as a group."

"I can't."

"I think you can. I've observed you your whole life, you know, and I've always found you strong enough to accept this life we have to live. Strong enough to make positive contributions to it. As you must now."

"But I love you!"

"And I love you. Just as I love all of you. And I'm doing the best I can to ensure a future for all of—" She turned and threw up again into the bucket.

Pete left her there. He thought of waking Jenna to help her, but Jenna was with the babies and anyway McAllister never needed help. She was that stone in Darlene's otherwise baffling song "Rock of Ages." It was Pete who needed help, but nobody was going to give him any, that was for sure.

He thought of volunteering for the next Grab, which was supposed to be Terrell's if he wasn't sick again, and deliberately getting himself killed. Then they'd be sorry! He thought of hitting Ravi over the head with the DIGITAL FOTO FRAME until Ravi was dead and then sending his body outside through the funeral slot before anyone even knew he was missing. They'd never suspect Pete. He thought of taking water and a shit bucket and going to live in his secret room, refusing to talk to anybody, just sneaking out at night to the farm to eat raw soy.

"Pete!" Caity yelled at him. "You left Petra on the

floor in the middle of the corridor! What were you *doing?*"

She held Petra, whose screaming had woken everyone. Kids cried or peered through the archway of the children's room. Terrell looked out from the Grab room, on duty to watch for brightening. Darlene bustled from her room, her bitter mouth turned down, her eyes still puffy from sleep. "You know them babies don't leave the children's room, Pete! What the hell were you doing?"

Tommy darted through the archway and wordlessly held out the DIGITAL FOTO FRAME. "Keep it," Pete snarled. Why not? Everything was shit, anyway.

Tommy looked incredulous with joy. Caity stared. Petra yelled. Darlene scolded. Pete's heart hurt so bad he thought it would burst right there in his chest, like some rotten protein-rich soy nut too spoiled to eat.

From down the hall Terrell cried, "The Grab is brightening! I'm going, everybody!"

APRIL 2014

JULIE GRUNTED and screamed on her living room floor. She lay in a pool of her waters. Her insides were trying to burst free of her body. The pain was incredible.

Jake, kneeling helplessly beside her, said, "I still think we should go to the hospital."

Between contractions, she glared at him; almost she spat at him. The hospital! She couldn't move, couldn't do anything but push. She gasped, "I'm shitting a pumpkin here!"

"But at the hospital—"

She screamed again and he shut up.

It wasn't supposed to happen like this. Last night Jake had flown in from Wyoming, arriving a full week before she was supposed to go into labor. He would drive her to the hospital and then wait decorously in the waiting room. Linda would coach Julie in the labor room. The first baby, her OB had assured her, always took a long time to come; Julie might even have false labor pains, similar to Braxton-Hicks contractions but "a little bit more intense," for several days. The baby nurse would come every day for two weeks after Julie came home from the hospital. It was all meticulously planned.

Then came these sudden, wrenching pains that woke her in the middle of the night; apparently she was already many more centimeters dilated than she should be because now the pumpkin was moving inexorably through her body, trying to kill her. Julie writhed and screamed, Jacob's terrified face looming over her. She would die, the baby would die, nobody could do this, *nobody*—

A final scream that brought neighbors pounding on the wall and a terrified oath from Jake. Linda, in a coat thrown over leopard-print pajamas, threw open the door and burst into the room. The pumpkin slid out and stopped torturing her, although everything on her still hurt and apparently always would. Julie burst into tears. The neighbor pounded harder. Jake cried, "What do I do now?" And the answering machine burst into life.

If the phone had been ringing, she hadn't heard it. But now she heard Gordon's voice, almost as if the relative cessation of pain had somehow created a pool of silence.

"Julie, this is Gordon. We've had another kidnapping. Three-year-old boy disappeared from his bed in southern Vermont. I remember that was on one of the projections you—"

Julie wasn't listening. Her baby had started to cry, and the sound filled the entire world, joyous and alive, leaving no room for anything else at all.

2035

PETE TRIED. McAllister had asked him to, so he did. He tried to be happy about her pregnancy. He tried to remember the good of all. He tried to be happy that Terrell's first Grab had brought back another child, even though it was a boy and not a girl. He tried to be pleasant to Caity while not having any more sex with her. He succeeded in none of these things, and both efforts and failure turned him very quiet.

"I like you better like this," Caity said after sex. "You don't talk."

Pete said nothing, turning his face away from her. They lay not in his secret room but in her bedroom at the other end of the Shell. Caity had taped to the wall another picture, this one torn from the box that had contained a toy. The actual toy, a doll, had been broken by some rambunctious child but the picture remained perfect: long body, tiny waist, big breasts, feet made in a permanent tiptoe. It looked nothing like any real woman Pete had ever seen, neither in the Shell nor on a Grab. Why had the Before people made dolls like that?

Terrell was disappointed that he hadn't Grabbed a girl. But McAllister said they should all be grateful that Terrell's first Grab had been so easy. Terrell had been able to get into the house, pick up the kid, and get out without waking anyone. McAllister named the boy "Keith," since he wouldn't, or couldn't, say his own name. "Never mind," Caity said. "Maybe McAllister's baby will be a girl."

"She's too old to be having a baby at all," Darlene said. "Pure foolishness. Probably we'll lose them both."

Pete stalked away, fists clenched at his side.

Caity had insisted she could handle another Grab—look how easy Terrell's was! She went and it did turn out to be easy, a store Grab in a "supermarket." Caity brought back a huge shopping cart of food and they had interesting feasts until it was gone, although the haul had not included any Reese's Peanut Butter Cups. The oversize shopping cart remained and was useful for hauling shit buckets. The next Grab would be Ravi's.

Pete spent a lot of time with Petra and Tommy, Petra because he wanted to, Tommy because he'd attached himself to Pete, pestering him about the promised "big adventure." Pete was harvesting soy in the farm, picking the thick ripe leaves and hard nuts, when Tommy started in again. Two half-full buckets sat on the floor beside the dirt beds. The farm smelled of rich dirt, growing crops, and the disinfectant waterfall by the fertilizer machine.

Tommy said, "When are we going on the adventure?"

"I don't know."

"What will it be?"

"You have to wait and see."

"I don't want to fucking wait."

"Don't let McAllister hear you using that language of Darlene's."

Tommy looked around fearfully as if McAllister might suddenly appear, then changed direction. "Why are those new grasses growing outside the Shell?"

This was no longer Pete's secret, just like nothing else was his, not even the DIGITAL FOTO FRAME. He said, "You know that, Tommy. You had it in learning circle. The Earth was sick but it's getting better."

"Why did it get sick?"

"The Tesslies did it. They destroyed the whole Earth."

"Why?"

"Because they're bastards."

"Oh. Why don't we kill them dead?"

"Because nobody but the Survivors has ever seen one, and that was a long time ago."

"Are the Tesslies going to come back?"

"I don't know."

Tommy considered this. "They have to come back, Pete, to let us out of the Shell."

"Maybe when it's time the Shell will just melt around us. You know, like the briar hedge in the fairy-tale book."

"Really? When?"

"McAllister says when the air is good to breathe again."

"Oh. When will that be?"

"I don't know, Tommy!"

Tommy said judiciously, "I don't think you know much."

Another voice behind Pete said, "You're right. He doesn't."

Ravi. Pete willed himself to not turn around. He was trying for the good of all, he was trying, he was *trying*. But Ravi these days had a cutting edge. McAllister had stopped having sex with him once she got pregnant; Pete knew this from Jenna, who'd been trying to make Pete feel better. At first Ravi swaggered and pretended that he and McAllister still did it. When Pete had smirked at him and rolled his eyes, Ravi had stalked away. After that he'd avoided Pete. Now he had come from the direction of McAllister's room, and Pete heard the dangerous note in his brother's voice, and knew that Ravi was as angry and frustrated as he was. And looking for a way to let that anger out.

Ravi repeated, "Pete doesn't know anything. He only thinks he does."

Tommy said, "Pete knows lots!"

"Really? I say he doesn't. Do you, Pete?"

Pete said nothing. Trying, trying, *trying!* Tommy, wide-eyed, looked back and forth between them.

Ravi pushed harder. "Pete doesn't know, for instance, how McAllister's breasts feel, do you, Pete?"

He knew he shouldn't. He knew a fight was what Ravi wanted, and that in giving it to him, Pete was losing. He even knew, somewhere in the back of his love-sick brain, what McAllister had said: *The biggest threat to any society is its own young males between the ages of fourteen and twenty-four*. None of it stopped him. In one fluid motion he grabbed the bucket of soy nuts and swung it at Ravi's head.

The bigger boy was unprepared. The edge of the bucket caught him in the mouth. Ravi cried out and went down, blood and teeth spurting onto the farm floor. Tommy screamed. Then Darlene was there, running from the other end of the farm, shrieking something about Cain and Abel.

Pete stared, horrified, at the writhing Ravi. "Is he dead? Is he dead?" Tommy cried, even though Ravi clearly was not. But he was hurt, badly hurt, all that blood, those *teeth*...

Then Pete was running down the corridor. For once Tommy didn't follow him. Pete hurled himself into the funeral room and pressed the button high on the wall; he had to jump to reach it. The slot opened, low on the opposite wall. Pete dropped to his knees and then onto his belly and crawled into it. The wall closed up behind him, and he was in darkness.

JUNE 2014

JULIE WALKED THE FLOOR of her living room with Alicia, now six weeks old. Despite being premature, Alicia had weighed a healthy six pounds at birth and just kept putting on weight, emptying Julie of milk as if she'd had a suction pump in her tiny pink mouth. Then, because she drank so fast, she got a tummy-ache and Julie had to walk her, steadily patting the baby's back, singing songs until Alicia burped, farted, threw up, or fell asleep. Tonight none of these things had yet happened. Julie paced up and down, caught as always in the rich stew of love, exasperation, fatigue, and joy that was motherhood. Behind her, CNN murmured softly. Sometimes the sound of the TV lulled Alicia into sleep. But not tonight.

Love, exasperation, fatigue, joy—but mostly love. Julie had never expected to feel such fierce, passionate, possessive attachment for anyone as she did for this damp, malodorous bundle on her shoulder. She'd always thought of herself as a cool person (in emotional temperature, not in hipness—she'd never been hip in her life). Certainly Gordon, nor any other man, had never ignited in her this intense love. Did he feel this way about his children? Did Linda about hers? Why hadn't anyone warned her?

"...continues in the clean-up efforts in Tokyo. Officials say it may be months before there is anywhere near a complete list of the dead. With damage reckoned in the billions and—" And there was the video again, shot from a tourist helicopter over Tokyo when the tsunami hit. The tsunami had registered 4.2 on the Soloviev-Imamura Intensity Scale, almost as large as the 2004 one in Indonesia. A wall of water ninety-four feet high had crashed over Tokyo.

"...not unexpected in that the Pacific Rim is well known for underwater faults that—"

Julie jiggled at the remote, trapped between Alicia's diaper and Julie's forearm. She got a rerun of M*A*S*H, then PBS: "—over 9,000 species going extinct each year, largely because of human activity. The rainforest is particularly susceptible as—" Another fumble at the remote, which fell to the floor. Unthinking, Julie bent to retrieve it. The sudden motion knocked a huge burp out of Alicia. She jerked in Julie's arms, let out a contented sigh, and went to sleep.

Don't think about the children drowned in Tokyo. There was nothing Julie could do about it. But standing there in the dim living room, she clutched her infant tight.

2035

As soon as the funeral slot closed up behind him, Pete wanted to get out again. In the complete darkness he pounded on the wall, all the walls. Nothing happened.

I always knew I would die this way, he thought, and immediately thought how stupid that was; he'd never had any such thought. He'd thought he would die on a Grab for the good of all, or from some sickness, or just old age. Or that he'd fight a Tesslie to both their deaths. But this—why didn't somebody else push the funeral button to let him out? Somebody would! Tommy would get someone tall enough, McAllister or Eduardo or Ravi...but Ravi lay bleeding on the farm floor with his teeth knocked out. Still, somebody must come soon...

The air went out of the dark room.

Pete heard it, in a whoosh, and then he couldn't breathe. Pain invaded his chest. So he would die here, he *would*—

Air rushed back in, and light, and Pete was shot forward by a force he couldn't see. It felt like someone had pushed him hard from behind. He landed beside Xiaobo, half-glimpsed through the rotting blanket, and a pile of bones.

Pete screamed and skittered away. Xiaobo was barely recognizable, a stinking mass of rotting flesh crawled over by disgusting white things. If it hadn't been for the little statue of the naked fat-bellied man on top of the mass, Pete wouldn't have known it was a human. But that was Xiaobo. Pete started to cry, then abruptly stopped.

He was Outside, but something was wrong with the air.

He could breathe it; this wasn't like the airless funeral slot. But the air was...*dirty*. He didn't know what he meant except that it was somehow not clean and fresh like the air in the Shell, but clogged with stuff he could smell and taste even if he couldn't see it. Still, it was air and he was breathing it and he was Outside.

Outside.

Partly to get away from Xiaobo and the other bones—which were Bridget's? Robert's? His father's?—Pete moved along the sides of the Shell. A plan formed in his dazed mind. He would find the clear patch of wall at the end of the Shell and he would wait there until Tommy or somebody went there and saw him. Then Pete would gesture to be let back in. McAllister could open the funeral slot and Pete could crawl past Xiaobo—ugh—back inside the Shell.

Unless—

He rounded the far edge of the Shell and forgot his plan.

The Shell sat on a hill of black rock. The black rock, broken with various grasses, sloped gently and unevenly a long way down, but then it gave way to... what? "Fields," McAllister had called them about his pictures in the DIGITAL FOTO FRAME. Not fields of amber grain like in Darlene's song, but of low, spindly bushes covered with green leaves. So many bushes that Pete felt dizzy. And none of them were soy! Beyond that were stretches of very tall grasses dotted with clumps of pink flowers and beyond those, more water than he had ever imagined still existed. It was blue water like on the beach where he had Grabbed Petra and Kara, water like Before!

He started to run down the hill, across the black rock toward the water. Pebbles and scrub crunched under his bare feet. Then something stopped him. At first he thought it was the hard-to-breathe air slowing him down, but this was more like someone had grabbed his arm from behind without him even feeling it. He turned, and there stood a Tesslie.

McAllister had described the alien over and over to the Six when they were younger: "In case you ever encounter one when I'm gone." At first Pete had thought she meant gone to use a shit bucket, or maybe to sleep, but when he grew older he knew she meant if she died. The Tesslie looked just as she had described: not a being but a hard metal case like a bucket, four feet high and squarish, with no head or mouth or anything. The bucket-case floated a few inches above the ground. Whatever the Tesslies were, they were inside. Or else this was a "robot," a machine like the battery-car from Jenna's Grab, and the Tesslie was controlling it from someplace else.

McAllister had said she didn't know which, and now Pete didn't know either.

"Aaaarggghhhh!" Pete cried and tried to leap on it, knock it over, split it open as he had split Ravi's mouth. This thing had killed his world!

He couldn't move. Not even a finger.

The Tesslie said nothing. But all at once Pete found it much harder to breathe. He wasn't breathing, he wasn't doing anything. He woke inside one of the tiny featureless rooms in the far end of the Shell, and it turned out that, in their concern over Ravi's injuries, no one even realized he'd been gone.

JUNE 2014

JULIE SAT IN FRONT of the young professor's desk. She didn't much like him, even though she'd only met him ten minutes ago. Pompous, self-satisfied, and perhaps even a little sleazy, or how else would he have the "top secret" information he claimed to possess? He'd made her sign a nondisclosure agreement, standard for her job, but still.... She didn't like him.

He said, "You come with top-level recommendations from people I'm not at liberty to name. You understand why not."

"Of course." He was name-dropping by not dropping any names, and he was out to make his own reputation. Nonetheless, curiosity was rising in her about the nature of the project for which he wanted predictive algorithms. He was a researcher in biology, after all—not usually the stuff of intense secrecy unless you were involved in genetic engineering or pharmaceutical research, which he was not. She'd checked him out. Two published articles so far, both on the geographical distribution of weeds nobody ever heard of, or cared about since the weeds were not edible, threatening, invasive, or endangered. The statistical analyses in both articles struck her as sloppy. But he was old money, Harvard, Skull and Crossbones—all the things that gave one contacts in high places.

His office was the usual thing for academics just starting to climb the university ladder: small, dark, crowded with metal shelves holding messy piles of papers, binders, fodders, books. A scuffed wooden desk and two chairs. Still, he wasn't housed in the building's basement with the teaching assistants, his office had a window, and on the wall hung an expensively framed photo of young men crewing on the Charles River.

Julie shifted on her chair. Beneath her maternity bra and thick sweater, she felt her breasts begin to leak. Alicia was a hungry little milk demon. Julie tried not to be away from her for more than a few hours at a time, for both their sakes.

Dr. Geoffrey Fanshaw pursed his lips theatrically, studied her, and nodded several times, as if making a decision that clearly had been made before. With a flourish suited to a bad Shakespearean actor, he handed her a sheaf of papers, then rose to lock his office door.

Ten minutes later Julie sat in shock, staring at him.

"How did you come by this information?"

"I told you that I can't say." He puffed with importance instead of what he should have felt: fear.

"The data on the simultaneous appearance of the altered *Klebsiella planticola* on three separate continents—you're sure of its authenticity?"

"Absolutely."

"And its accuracy?"

"Yes."

"Have you personally visited any of these sites? The Connecticut one, maybe?"

Annoyance erased his habitual smirk. "No, not yet. New Zealand and Brazil, of course, would be difficult to get to. And—"

"But," she burst out, unable to restrain herself, "what is anybody *doing* about this?"

"I don't know. My concern is publishing on-line with the predictive algorithms in place as soon as the story blows in the press. Which can't be too long now—some smart journalist will get it. As soon as that happens, I want to be poised to publish in a professional journal with some prominence."

Julie heard what Fanshaw wasn't saying: he wanted to be the instant go-to guy for the news shows, talk shows, sound-bite seekers. A professor, personable, well-connected, first to publish a serious analysis—he'd be a natural. He wanted the *60 Minutes* interview and the *Today* show discussion, and to hell with the fact that in three widely separated locations around the planet—three known about now, who was to say there weren't actually more—a deadly bacterial mutation was killing the roots of plants through an alcoholic by-product. Drowning them in booze. A bacterium found on the roots of virtually every plant on Earth except those growing in or near brackish water.

Fanshaw said eagerly, "Can you do the statistical analysis?"

She managed to get out, "Yes."

"By when? I need it, like, yesterday."

"I'll start this afternoon." The statistical part wasn't hard. There must be mathematicians—not to mention biologists!—working frantically on this around the globe. Fanshaw was right—the press would get this very soon. And if—

The fuller implications hit her.

"If this isn't natural—*three* locations for a naturally occurring identical mutation just doesn't seem likely. Even an accidental release of a created genetic mutation would only happen in one place. So is this a terrorist attack?"

"I don't know." For a second he looked almost concerned, but that washed away in a fresh surge of self-obsession. "As I said, Dr. Kahn, time is of the essence, I need those algorithms."

"Yes." She stood, unable to stand him one minute more.

On her way to the parking lot, breasts leaking milk with every step, she passed summer-term students hurrying to class, chatting on a low wall, sprawled on the grass over open books or laptops. Despite herself, she stopped to gaze at a flower bed, unable to look away. Pansies, impatiens, baby's breath.

Nearly every plant on Earth.

Who? And in the name of every god she didn't believe in—*why?*

2035

MCALLISTER AND TOMMY were the only ones who believed Pete had been Outside. Tommy was angry because Pete hadn't taken him along on the "adventure." McAllister was tense with hope. "Tell me again," she said.

They sat alone in her room. Pete avoided looking at the curve of her belly. Again he recited everything that had happened, too frightened at what he himself had done to leave anything out, not even the cause of the fight with Ravi. But that wasn't what she was interested in.

"You saw bushes and grasses. Trees?"

"No."

"Animals?"

"No."

"And you could breathe."

"It was a little hard."

"Like you weren't getting enough air?"

"Yeah. But not very bad." How could that be? There had been air all around him, blowing gently as it never did inside the Shell.

She guessed the question he wasn't asking. "You had trouble breathing because the air mix still isn't right out there. Maybe there's too much CO_2—the destruction of the Earth's forests would have really screwed up the oxygen-carbon dioxide balance. Maybe too many volcanic particles still, maybe toxins, maybe too much methane. I don't know. I wasn't an ecologist. But I think the atmosphere was becoming unbreathable when the Tesslies put us into the Shell. And now *you* could breathe it."

"Does that mean they'll let us out soon?"

McAllister raised both hands, let them drop, screwed up her face. Her pregnancy had made her more emotional, which everyone had observed and Pete did not understand. Was that usual? "Pure foolishness, getting herself knocked up at her age," Darlene had said. "Who does she think she is, Abraham's Sarah?" Caity bit her lip and looked away every time McAllister waddled into a room. Pete was just glad he wasn't female.

McAllister said, "How should I know what the Tesslies will do?"

Pete burst out, "I'll kill them if I can!"

She didn't answer that; they both knew it was too ridiculous. Instead she said yet again, "And you couldn't tell if the Tesslie was a living being inside a space suit or a robot."

"I don't know."

She smiled. "Neither did I, the one time I saw one."

"How did it *get* here?"

"I don't know, dear heart. Until the Grab machinery appeared, I assumed they'd all left Earth after putting us Survivors in the Shell. After all, nobody had seen one for twenty years. But either they returned or else they were observing us all along."

Pete had known they watched him! Fucking bastards—

McAllister said, "Thank you, Pete. You can go now, but later I want to talk to you and Ravi together."

"I've got Grab duty."

"Do you want someone else to take it?"

"No." He made himself ask, "Is Ravi all right?"

"He will be."

She looked very tired. Pete said awkwardly, "Are *you* all right? With…everything?"

"I'm fine. I'm just a little old to be doing this."

Well, you didn't have to! But Pete didn't say it. He blundered out and went to the Grab room.

Staring at the inert Grab machinery, which might brighten but probably wouldn't, Pete thought about his own questions. The air outside was breathable. It wasn't really good, but it was breathable enough. What was "enough"? There were bushes and grasses and—yes, he remembered now, wrenching the picture into his mind as if yanking up a pair of pants— berries. There had been red berries on some of the bushes. Almost he turned back to tell McAllister, but he didn't want to face her again.

He had no choice. Somewhere during his Grab duty she came in with Ravi. Immediately Pete wanted to be somewhere else. He got to his feet, scowling to cover his confusion.

Ravi's mouth was all swollen. His two top front teeth were broken off into jagged stumps. Pete had a moment of panic—how would Ravi eat? Well, he still had all his other teeth.... But his good looks were badly marred. Even without all the puffy swelling, Ravi was never again going to look like the handsome princes in the fairy-tale book.

McAllister said, "Both of you men were at fault in this fight, but—" For a minute Pete didn't listen, caught by her referring to them as "men." Had McAllister ever done that before? When he heard her again, it was clear she was blaming him more than Ravi, because "...violence. Not only is it never needed to settle disputes, it damages the good of all and sets a terrible example for the children. Pete, you wouldn't want Tommy or Petra to someday behave as you did today, would you?"

Pete couldn't imagine Petra behaving any way at all except smiling or wailing or kicking her fat little legs. Too far in the future. But he saw what McAllister meant, and hung his head.

She was talking to Ravi now. "What you were doing, looking to start a fight with Pete because you were angry with me, is something all humans have to struggle against all the time. Do you understand, Ravi? Winning that struggle with ourselves will be a huge part of what lets us successfully restart humanity. Do you understand that?"

"Yes," Ravi said. Pete couldn't tell if Ravi meant it or not. His voice came out mangled through the swollen mouth.

"You two are brothers," McAllister said passionately, "and I know that your biological parents, Richard and Emily and Samir, would not have wanted you to act the way you did today. But even more than brothers, you are members of this colony, with a mission that others have already struggled and died for. You must work together no matter what for our survival, or all those other deaths are wasted."

Ravi said something. McAllister didn't understand the garbled words; she leaned forward and said, "What?" Ravi shook his head.

But Pete had heard. Ravi had said, "Kill Tesslies." That was what Ravi thought was their "mission." And Pete did, too! His head snapped up to look at Ravi, who gazed back. Something passed between them, and all Pete's animosity vanished. They had a joint mission: revenge. That was more important than who had sex with McAllister, who anyway wasn't looking very attractive with her belly swollen in pregnancy and all those tired lines around her eyes.

Ravi nodded. They understood each other. McAllister beamed.

"Good," she said. "Now shake hands."

They did, and Pete squeezed his brother's hand. They were on the same side again. They would be killers together.

McAllister said, "I'm so happy."

Both of them smiled at her.

JUNE 2014

ALONG THE EUPHRATES river grew a strip of green: trees, grass, flowers. Away from the river the land turned more arid, dotted with scrub grazed on by sheep and goats. Here, not far from where Babylon had once stood, bacteria mutated on the tap long root of a plant.

2035

PETE AND RAVI were now allies. Together they were going to get revenge for Earth. The first Tesslie they saw—and one had to show up eventually, after all Pete had seen one when he'd gone Outside!—they were going to kill.

A week after the fight they sat in the clear-walled room, gazing out at the growing grasses in the black rock. "Those are taller than yesterday," Ravi said.

"Yeah," Pete said, although to him the grasses looked exactly the same height. Pete felt obliged to agree with most of what Ravi said because with Ravi's swollen mouth and broken teeth, Ravi's words came out a little garbled. On the other hand, he still had his greater height and bigger muscles, which saved Pete from feeling as bad as he would otherwise. The fight had merely evened things up, he felt, the way Darlene "evened up" blankets when she folded them. The same for both sides. Still, Pete sometimes wished that he and Ravi had had the same father, not the same mother. Ravi's build came from his father Samir, whom Pete could just remember, unlike both of his own parents.

"When we find a Tesslie," Ravi mumbled—it was always *when*, not *if*—"we should have a plan. I'll grab it from behind and you—"

"Wait a minute," Pete said. "Is the Tesslie an alien inside a bucket-case or a robot?"

"Does it matter?"

"Yes! If it's a robot, then you hold it and I'll find the battery case, open it, and pull out the batteries."

"Good, good," Ravi said. "If it's an alien inside a bucket-case, then I'll hold it tight, you find the place where the bucket-case opens and unbutton or unzip or pry it apart or whatever. Then we can drag the bastard out and hit it with something."

"With what?" Pete said.

Ravi considered. "We should have a weapon all ready. Hidden, but someplace where we can get at it quick when we need it. I know! Those metal-toed boots from that Grab!"

Pete nodded enthusiastically. The boots were never worn; who wanted all that weight? In the Shell everyone went barefoot. Pete had never seen the point of them. But as a weapon…

Ravi said, "We can kick the Tesslie with those boots and stomp on it until it's all bloody!"

Pete frowned. The vivid picture created by Ravi's words didn't look as appealing as before Ravi described it. Ravi, however, went on and on, spouting things they could do to the Tesslie.

Partly to stop him, partly because the thought had been growing in him for some time, Pete said, "Ravi, I have another idea."

"What?"

"I think it would help us if we understood more about how Tesslie machinery works. In case, you know, the Tesslies *are* machinery. We should pick one piece of it and take it apart, examine it real good, then put it back together before McAllister even knows we did it."

Ravi's mouth fell open, fully exposing his broken teeth. "Take it apart?"

"Yes. For information about the Tesslies."

"What if…what if we can't get the machinery back together again?"

"We'll be careful, go slow, look at each piece in great detail." They were words Jenna had used about McAllister's lesson in taking apart and cleaning McAllister's precious microscope. Pete wasn't allowed near the microscope, not since that business with the shit bucket and the broken glass slide.

Ravi said, "Well, if you're sure…"

"I am," said Pete, who wasn't. But all at once the project seemed the most fascinating thing he'd ever done. Find out more about the Tesslies, the better to defeat them! He was like the Little Tailor in the fairy-tale book, using his brain to triumph over evil giants.

"What machinery do we take apart?"

"Well," Pete said, thinking it out as he spoke, "there are only five Tesslie machines in the Shell. The Grab platform—"

"We can't risk *that*," Ravi said.

"—and the funeral slot and the fertilizer machine and the main waterfall and the disinfectant waterfall.

I think the funeral slot."

"No, the fertilizer machine! Then if we can't get it back together, we won't have to do shit-bucket duty anymore!"

"And the shit will just pile up inside the Shell," Pete said. Sometimes Ravi didn't think things through. "The funeral slot is better. Nobody else is sick enough to die. Anyway, I don't think it will be as hard as the other machines. When I was inside the slot, I could see some pipes or something overhead before it got completely dark."

"Pete, did you really go—*look at that!*"

Pete's head snapped around. Outside the Shell, something streaked past, too fast for him to see. "What was it? What was it?"

"I don't know? Maybe...a cat!"

"There are no cats, not in houses or stores," Pete said, with an authority he didn't feel. He'd never seen a cat except in the books. Why did Ravi and not him get to see the not-cat?

"Something like a cat, then! I don't know! But it was alive!"

They both pressed their faces to the clear part of the Shell, but the thing didn't reappear. Finally Pete said sulkily, "*Yes*, I went Outside—I told you! So let's start on that funeral slot. You go get the flashlight and some rope and...and a bucket. A big one."

"What for?"

"You'll see."

Ravi obeyed him, which made Pete feel a little better. Next time, *he* would see the not-cat.

In the funeral room, Pete worked slowly. It was a pleasure to not have to hurry, hurry, hurry like on a Grab. He put the bucket close to the slot, the rope in his hand, the flashlight, usually stored in the children's room for an emergency that had never come, in his teeth. Then he had to take it out again to explain to Ravi what was going to happen.

"You press the button to open the slot, and I'll go in. Then you jam the bucket in the slot so it can't close up again. I'll study the machinery above my head in the slot, and if I see something we want for a closer look, I'll tie the rope around it and use that to yank it out."

"Why do you get to go? I want to go, too! The slot is big enough for both of us if we squeeze."

It was, although just barely. Although Pete didn't like the idea of being jammed that close to Ravi.

Ravi added, "It's only fair that I get to go in the slot, too. You already had a turn! You went all the way Outside!"

"I thought you didn't even believe me about that! And stop whining!"

"I'm not whining!"

Glaring at each other, they got into position. Ravi pressed the button. Pete scooted in. Ravi jammed the bucket into the opening and then crawled past it so that he and Pete lay side by side on their backs. The flashlight was necessary because their bodies blocked nearly all the light coming from the funeral room. Pete swept the beam over the ceiling a foot above them.

The Tesslie machinery wasn't pipes after all, as he had originally thought. It was hard to say what it was. Rounded bumps, irregular indentations, two protrusions shaped vaguely like small bowls. These were easiest to tackle. Pete looped the rope around one. "I'm going to pull on this, just a little bit."

Ravi said, "I want to go Outside."

"Ravi! That's not what we're doing! Besides, I promised McAllister I wouldn't do that again."

"*I* didn't promise her that. And you had a turn Outside so it's only fair that I do. How do I get the other door to open?"

"Ravi, no, it won't open until you—"

Ravi kicked away the bucket.

Pete tried to hit him but there was no room to swing his fist. Pete took a huge gulp of air, knowing what would come next: the air whooshing out of the slot, the outer door sliding open to push him and Ravi out on top of Xiaobo's rotting body... Let Ravi get his own air!

Nothing happened.

The boys lay in the glow from the flashlight. The air did not leave the chamber; Pete could hear Ravi's breathing. Finally Ravi said in a small voice, "When does it open?"

"It isn't going to, you fucker! The Tesslies must have changed the machine! We're trapped!" All at once Pete, who had never minded small spaces before (but when had he ever been in one this small?) felt his heart speed up. Sweat sprang onto his forehead, his palms. Frantically he jostled Ravi, trying to get more space, get more air, *get out…*

"Ow!" Ravi said. "Stop it! Hey, everybody in the Shell, we're trapped inside the funeral slot! Terrell! Tommy! Caity! Hey!"

Pete joined him in screaming. He yelled until his throat hurt. How thick was that slot wall? What if no one ever came?

After what seemed days, weeks, Pete heard a voice on the other side of the wall: "Lord preserve us—ghosts!"

"It's Darlene," Ravi whispered hoarsely.

Darlene began to howl one of her songs. "'Save us from ghosts and demons that—'"

"Darlene! It's not ghosts or demons, it's Pete and Ravi! We're trapped in here! Let us out!"

The howling stopped. Darlene said, "Pete?"

"Yes! Press the funeral button!"

Silence. Then Darlene's voice again but closer, as if she now squatted close to the low slot. "You want to come out?"

"Yes!" Of course they wanted to come out—why did it have to be crazy Darlene that found them?

She said, "I'll let you out after you repent of your sins. You, Pete—you say you're a sinner for sassing me and for disobedience and for setting yourself above your elders!"

Pete's teeth came together so fast and hard that he bit his lip. Ravi snapped, "Do it! Or she'll never let us out!"

He could wait for someone else, anyone else. But now that escape was at hand, the thought of waiting even one unnecessary minute longer in this place was intolerable. Pete snarled, "All right! I repent of my sins!"

"Name them!" Darlene said.

"I repent of sassing you and disobedience and setting myself up above my elders!"

"Now you, Ravi. You repent of fornication with McAllister, who is another generation, and of sassing me and disobedience."

Ravi yelled, "I repent! Open the fucking slot!"

"That ain't true repentance, but I'll take it. Now both of you sing with me a cleansing hymn of—"

"What is going on here?"

McAllister's voice. Pete's heart leapt and then sank, a reversal so quick it left him gasping. Ravi yelled, "McAllister, Pete and I are in here! Let us out!"

The slot slid upwards. Pete and Ravi scuttled out on their backs. Pete felt dizzy. Blood streamed down his chin from his bitten lip. McAllister stared down at the flashlight in his hand, the rope trailing out behind him, the bucket on the floor. From this angle, her belly jutted out like a shelf. Pete had never seen that look on McAllister's face. He felt four years old again, except that no adult but Darlene ever glared like that at a four-year-old.

Ravi, the great lover, hung his head. In a tiny voice he said, "I saw a cat outside, McAllister, running past the Shell. Really. I did."

JUNE 2014

GEOFFREY FANSHAW did not get the notoriety he'd hoped for.

Julie finished the analysis he wanted and sent it to him. She expected to hear back from him, but— nothing. On reflection, she decided she'd been dumb to expect acknowledgement. She had served her purpose to Fanshaw and he had discarded her; that was what narcissists did. She was left with his check and her own fears.

At night she dreamed of plants dying, all over the world.

Two more jobs came her way, and she took them both. Around the consulting work she fit a separate, obsessive routine: Wake at 5:00 a.m. Coffee, banishing the lingering night dreams with wake-up caffeine. Care for Alicia. Bundle the baby into her pram and, before the streets of D.C. got too hot, make the long walk to World Wide News to buy newspapers. The *Washington Post*, the *New York Times*: the on-line versions left too much out. Also a host of small-town papers. The rest of the day she stayed inside, bathed in the air conditioning that divided her and Alicia from the steaming D.C. summer. She worked and then she read, barely glancing at the wide variety of usual disasters available in the world:

FOREST FIRES OUT OF CONTROL IN BRAZIL

MAN KILLS WIFE, SELF

ECOLOGICAL BALANCE SEVERELY THREATENED BY OVER-GRAZING

ILLEGAL STRIP MINING CAUSES ARMED STAND-OFF WITH LAW

She was looking for something unusual, and she would know it when she found it. No, not "it"— "them." She searched for two things, and on the first day of July she finally found one of them. Only a small item far inside the *Times*, bland and inoffensive:

SCIENTISTS SOLVE PLANT MYSTERY

A team of scientists led by Dr. Simon Langford of the U.S. Department of Agriculture announced that the "mystery plague" affecting plants along the Connecticut shoreline has been stopped. "It was a random, natural mutation in one specific microbe," Langford said, "but relatively easy to contain and kill off with appropriate chemicals. No mystery, really."

A section of shoreline in the Connecticut Wetlands Preserve has been closed to the public for several days while the botanical correction was carried out. Preserve officials announced that the wetlands will remain closed for the near future, "for further monitoring, as a purely precautionary measure." Disappointed tourists were turned away by Security personnel but given free passes to other local attractions.

"This sort of thing happens routinely," Langford concluded. "We're on top of it."

"Bullshit," Julie said aloud to Alicia, who gurgled back.

It was a cover-up—but why? And of what?

Julie knew, or thought she knew, but she didn't want to know. Not yet. She could be wrong, it was a fancifully dumb idea, in fact it skirted the edges of insanity. Just one of those stray ideas that crossed the mind but meant nothing....

She read the bland article again, then stared out her apartment window at a tree, carefully enclosed in a little wrought-iron fence, growing where a section of city sidewalk had been meticulously removed to accommodate it.

2035

ALL AT ONCE the Grab machinery went crazy.

Ravi was on duty. He and Pete had been talked to by McAllister, a talk that left both of them near tears. She wasn't angry, she was disappointed. Angry would have been better. Not even Ravi's sighting of the not-cat outside had deterred McAllister from her disappointment. Pete wasn't sure that McAllister even believed Ravi. Pete wasn't sure he did, either. When McAllister was finished with them, Pete and Ravi avoided each other for a week—until Ravi was restored to puffed-up triumph by his amazing Grab.

"I was all ready," he later told everyone, although Pete had his doubts about that—why even bother to repeat it over and over unless it wasn't true? And Ravi had a history of falling asleep during Grab-room duty. But whether he had leaped onto the platform at first brightening, or had just barely caught the Grab before it went away, it was irrefutable that Ravi had gone. He had gone close-mouthed both because of McAllister's scolding and because he was embarrassed by the lack of the teeth that Pete had knocked out, but he returned smiling wide. His shout had reached both the children's room and the farm. Pete, on crop duty with Darlene, had run toward the Grab room, along with everyone else.

Ravi stood on the platform behind the biggest pile of *stuff* that Pete had ever seen. It almost hid Ravi; it spilled off the edges of the platform; it clanked and clattered as it fell. Pete couldn't even identify half of it. How could even Ravi, the strongest of them all, load all this in ten minutes? And onto what?

McAllister, running clumsily behind the bulk of her pregnancy, stopped in the doorway. She went still and white.

"Look what I got!" Ravi shouted. "Look!"

"What is it all?" Caity said. She held a child in each arm. "How did you *bring* it all?"

"The Grab stayed open for more than ten minutes— for twenty-two minutes! It was a store Grab and I got this big rolling thing—see, it's under all this—and just piled things on. There only was this kind of stuff, so that's what I took. But look how much of it!" Ravi practically swelled with pride. *Bloated*, Pete thought. Like when someone was diseased in their belly.

Why couldn't Pete have been the one to bring back the big haul? Whatever it was.

McAllister finally spoke. "Twenty-two minutes?"

"I timed it," Ravi said proudly.

Caity repeated, "What is it all? What's that thing with the skinny metal spikes coming out of it?"

"A rake," McAllister said. Then it seemed that once she started talking, she couldn't stop. "A rake, several hoes, bags of seed and fertilizer, trowels, flower seeds, hoses, flower pots, wind chimes—*wind chimes!*"

Pete had never seen McAllister like this—wild-eyed, hysterical—not even when he and Ravi had gotten trapped in the funeral slot. Fear pricked him. But the next moment she had recovered herself.

"You were in a garden store, Ravi. And you did well. Let's get this stuff off the rolling cart so we can get the cart down off the platform. Caity, take Karim and Tina back to the children's room, and on your way get Darlene to help Jenna with the children. She'll have to do it because we need you here. Tommy, go wake up Eduardo. Terrell, you and Ravi and Pete start moving this stuff. We need that platform clear right away."

"Why?" Pete said.

"I don't know yet. Let's just do it."

Caity ran down the corridor with the kids. Pete leaped forward to help unload the platform. If McAllister was ordering Darlene to help with the children, then something important was going on.

They got all the stuff off the platform, including the long, heavy rolling cart. Immediately Terrell jumped on it and Ravi pushed him out the room and down the corridor. Terrell laughed delightedly. "I want a ride, too!" Caity cried, running after the cart.

The platform glowed.

Pete gaped at it. It never brightened again so soon after a Grab—never!

McAllister said, in a voice somehow not her own, "Go." She handed Pete the wrister that Ravi had turned over to her.

Pete hopped onto the platform, the laughter from the corridor still ringing in his ears.

JUNE 2014

JULIE CONTINUED to read the papers obsessively: "STAR-VATION REACHES CRITICAL POINT IN SOMALIA." "OVERPOPULATION BIGGEST THREAT TO PLANET." But nothing more was mentioned about the mutated bacteria, not anywhere in the world. Nor could she find anything on-line. If the story about *K. planticola* was being repressed, several countries must be cooperating in doing that, by every means available. The completeness of the suppression was almost as scary as the microbial mutation.

Almost.

Several times she picked up the phone to call Fanshaw's office. Each time she laid it down again. If there *was* a cover-up going on, if there really were scientists and covert organizations and high officials in several countries working to keep this from the public, then Julie did not want to call any attention to herself. Fanshaw had probably, given his narcissism, erased any trace of help from anybody else in crafting the article he never got to publish. He would, of course, have preserved her nondisclosure agreement, and Julie could only hope he had it in a safe, secret place. But he had also written her a check "For professional services," and she had cashed it.

She Googled him. Until two weeks ago he had been all over the Net. Then his posts on Facebook ceased, as did his blog.

"You seem preoccupied," Linda said. They sat under an awning in her back yard, drinking cold lemonade and watching Linda's three kids splash in the pool. Alicia lay asleep in her infant seat. The beach-cottage-in-August scheme had been dropped; Linda and Ted were taking the children to visit their grandmother in Winnipeg, where it was twenty-five degrees cooler.

"I'm sorry," Julie said.

"Everything all right? The consulting?"

"Going better than I'd dared hope. And I'm making a lot more money than I was teaching."

"Well, I can see that Alicia's all right. So...Ju, is it Gordon? I know he called the night Alicia was born. You were on the floor with Jake, I burst in, and Gordon's voice was coming from your answering machine."

Linda had never mentioned this before. It had been two days before Julie even listened to Gordon's message: *"We've had another kidnapping. A three-year-old boy taken from his bed in southern Vermont."*

She said to Linda, "He called about the work project. You know I can't discuss it with you."

"I know. Spook stuff. But that wasn't all he said. At the end his voice changed completely when he said, 'Are you all right?' Have you seen him since? Do you miss him? Is that why you seem so...not here?"

Julie put her hand, cold from the lemonade glass,

over her friend's. "No, I haven't seen him. And no, I don't miss him. Sometimes I feel guilty about that, like it proves I'm a shallow person."

Linda grinned. "You're not that. Still waters, brackish but deep."

"Thanks. I think." And then, before she knew she was going to say it, "Linda, did you ever read James Lovelock?"

"No. Who's he?"

"It doesn't matter. Do you believe...do you think there are things about the universe that we can't explain? Things that lie so far beyond science they're something else entirely?"

"I lapsed from Catholicism when I was fourteen," Linda said, "and never saw any reason to unlapse. Ju, have you suddenly got religion?"

"No, no, nothing like that. It's not anything, really. Just the heat."

"Yeah, I can't wait until we leave for—Colin! If you do that one more time you're getting out of the pool, do you hear me?"

Alicia woke. Colin did that one more time. Normal life, routine and mundane as precious as the propagation of plants.

JULY 2014

It wasn't dark, and it wasn't light. It wasn't anything except cold. *I'm dead*, Pete thought, but of course he wasn't. Then he was through and the ocean lay to his right, just as it had all those months ago when he'd Grabbed Petra and Kara. But this beach was smaller than the other, a strip of stony ground jammed between sea and a sort of little cliff. Big rocks jutting out of the water as well as the land. Also, the air was warmer and lighter. In fact, for the first time ever, the Grab seemed to be happening in full daylight. The sun shone brightly halfway above the horizon— so brightly that Pete blinked at it, momentarily patterning his vision with weird dots.

When they cleared, he saw the little house on the top of the cliff above him. There seemed to be no path up. Cursing, Pete climbed, hands and feet seeking holds in the rock, some of which crumbled under his grip. Once he nearly fell. But he made it to the top and stood, his back against the house, to look at his wrister.

Five minutes gone.

The sea below him lay smooth as the mirror Caity had Grabbed long ago. Sunlight reflected off it, enveloping everything in a silver-blue glow. Pete wasted precious seconds staring at the beauty; it made good fuel for his hatred. When he and Ravi eventually found Tesslies...

No time now for revenge pictures.

The house had long since lost all its paint to the salt winds. A window, small and too high for Pete to peer into, stood open, but he heard no sounds coming from within. Cautiously he rounded the corner of the house.

It stood on a point jutting above the ocean, and now he had a new angle on the path down to the beach below. Two figures walked there, away from the house, holding hands. They stopped briefly to kiss, then moved on. Pete moved to the front door of the cottage.

It stood open. The screen door, with a metal screen so old and soft that it felt like cloth under his hands, was unlocked. Pete slipped into a tiny hall-way, cool after the bright sun outside. He could see clear through to the back of the house, which was all glass with yet another view of the sea. All the rooms were small, to fit the house on the narrow point. To his left was a kitchen, to the right a steep staircase. Pete climbed it.

Two little bedrooms, both with slanted walls and windows set into alcoves. One room held a double bed and a long, low dresser. Crowded into the other were a crib and a single bed, both occupied.

She was the most beautiful girl he'd ever seen, more beautiful even than McAllister. Pete gaped at her long red hair—he hadn't known hair could be that color!—her smooth golden skin, her sweetly curved body and long legs. She wore a thin white top and panties, and nearly everything was on display. Something about her attitude suggested that she had only recently flung herself onto the bed and had fallen instantly asleep. It was a few moments before he could even look into the crib.

When he did, he found a miniature of the girl. Not plump and smooth like Petra, this child looked delicate, graceful, like the fairies in *The Illustrated Book of Fairy Tales*. When Pete lifted her, he scarcely felt her weight, not even on his weak arm. Neither the baby nor her gorgeous sister woke.

Could he bring the older girl back, too? Pete gazed down at her. The rules of the Grab were strict, except that no one knew what they were. Everyone above a certain age died going through the Grab—but what age? Robert had died going through, at thirty-nine, Seth at forty-two. Petra's father had died, at who knew what age. Pete could still go through at fifteen. Where between fifteen and thirty-nine was the death age? How old was this girl?

Pete couldn't risk it. A lingering look at the redhead and he crept downstairs with the baby.

Twelve minutes had passed. If he had the same twenty-two minutes as Ravi, then he had to wait ten more minutes. But maybe he didn't have ten more—who knew what the Tesslies would do? Other than watch humans squirm and struggle to survive. When he and Ravi caught one—not *if*, when—they would—

Chime chime chime...

The doorbell! Pete looked frantically around for somewhere to hide. But it wasn't the doorbell, it was a clock sitting on a table made of tree branches painted white. *Chime chime chime...*

The girl upstairs screamed.

Pete looked frantically around. Nothing to hide behind, or under... He sprinted for the hall. Before he could reach the front door, the girl came tearing down the stairs. Pete ran into the kitchen. A door stood open and he darted inside, closing it behind him. The girl went on screaming, an incoherent mix of words; if she was calling the baby's name, Pete couldn't decipher it.

Through all of this, the baby hadn't awakened. Pete couldn't see his wrister in the darkness of the pantry. But he could smell food all around him. Cautiously he shifted the baby to his shoulder and felt around with his free hand. When it closed on a package of something, he clasped it to the baby and felt for another.

Now the door slammed; the girl had gone outside. A moment later she was back, tearing upstairs and then down again, still screaming but this time as if talking to someone. "My sister my baby sister Susie she's gone! I was asleep—I *can't* calm down don't you understand you moron Susie is gone! Taken! I was— they're walking the beach and—1437 Beachside Way and—yes I'm sure some fucking bastard took her!"

Pete heard McAllister's voice in his head, "Not that language, Pete. I know Darlene uses it but it's not a good example for the kids." *Fucking bastard*. The beautiful, beautiful girl was talking about Pete with the same words Pete talked about Tesslies.

For the first time, he thought about the people left behind when he took their children. How they must feel.

Why hadn't he ever thought about that before? Why hadn't McAllister made him think about it? Did Caity or Ravi or Jenna or Terrell? Maybe Jenna did. But Pete had only thought about getting back home safely with the Grabbed kids, about how important it was to restart humanity.

Well, it was! And that was how McAllister always said it. Restarting humanity and saving the Grab children from the Tesslie destruction of the Earth. It was a heroic thing to do, and Pete was a hero for doing it.

The girl on the other side of the pantry door threw something hard against the kitchen wall and again slammed the screen door, screaming, "Mom! Dad! Where the fuck are you!"

Still the baby slept. Pete felt around again on the pantry shelves. He found another package of something, then yet another. Then the Grab caught him, and he was back on the platform with the slumbering baby, two packages of penne pasta, and a loaf of whole wheat bread with rosemary and dill.

"Oh!" Tommy cried. "A baby!"

Everyone clustered around the platform to greet

him and take the infant, and even Caity smiled at him. Even Darlene. Pete smiled back. Jauntily he jumped down and handed the baby to McAllister.

Behind him, the Grab platform brightened again.

JULY 2014

JUST PAST MIDNIGHT Julie, seated in front of her computer, put her hands to her face and pulled at the skin hard, trying to fully wake herself up. Today—no, yesterday—was her thirty-ninth birthday. Jake had called from Wyoming. Linda, in the midst of packing her family for Winnipeg, had dashed over with a chocolate cake with a mini-forest of candles. It had been a good day and Julie should have been in bed reliving it in dreams, but instead she'd sat at her computer for four and a half hours, flipping between news sites and screens full of data.

She almost had it, the right algorithm.

She could smell it, tantalizing as apples in October. But this was not autumn and this particular apple evoked Snow White's Wicked Witch, Alan Turing's cyanide-laced fruit, the serpent in the Garden of Eden.

God, she was beyond tired, or her thoughts wouldn't turn so metaphorical. It wasn't as if there weren't enough to fear without figurative exaggeration.

Three more data points. One she felt certain about:

the kidnapping in Vermont on the night Alicia was born. A three-year-old boy had vanished from his bedroom while his parents were out at a party. Local cops had his baby-sitter, a Dominican woman who barely spoke English, in custody. She swore she had been asleep on the living room sofa when the abduction occurred; undoubtedly they assumed she was lying. Julie knew she was not.

The other two data points were more uncertain. A break-in in a garden shop in Massachusetts, no forced entry, the cash box untouched. The usual bizarre collection of goods had been taken: rakes, seeds, wind chimes. And yesterday's incident, the kidnapping of a Maine infant who was supposedly being watched by her teenage sister while the parents strolled on the beach. No trace of the baby girl had been found, but the whole thing so closely resembled a set-up that even the local cops were suspicious, regarding the sister as either a suspect or a scapegoat; Julie couldn't tell which. Could be a significant, could not. The location fit with her current algorithm, but not so closely if she didn't include it as a data point to create the algorithm in the first place, which was the kind of thinking that drove mathematicians crazy. And when had she started thinking of a lost child as a "data point"?

She had to go to bed. Just one more scan of breaking news. And there it was:

SCIENTIST ARRESTED FOR SECURITY BREACH

Dr. Geoffrey Fanshaw, Biologist,
Believed Connected to
Unspecified Terrorist Activity

The article said nothing much. It didn't have to. Julie, all exhaustion banished, ran into her bedroom and started packing.

2035

Two Grabs right in a row, then nothing for a few days, then another Grab for Caity.

They're playing fucking games, ain't they," Darlene said. "With our lives!"

"Not yours," Caity answered spitefully. "*You* never have to go." She was disappointed with the results of her Grab. She'd found herself in a strange, small store for twenty-two minutes and had not known what to do. There were no shopping carts, and anyway she was afraid of this store. She hadn't said that, not even later, but then Caity didn't ever admit fear. Still, Pete knew that's what she'd felt. She hadn't wanted to touch anything, but neither did she want to come back empty-handed and anyway, she said later and in a strong temper, "Who knew what the fuck McAllister was going to want?" So she yanked some zippered carrying-bags off a shelf and made herself stuff things into them.

"Gerbils?" Eduardo said, astonished. He and Tommy happened to walk by the Grab room just as Caity returned.

"That's what they had!" Caity was near tears. "Get McAllister! Never mind, I'll go myself!"

139

"Wow, a puppy!" Tommy cried, unzipping a bag with mesh sides.

The Six had never seen gerbils before. Only Terrell, Jenna, and Pete had seen dogs during Grabs, and the one Pete saw had tried to kill him. He didn't much like the puppy, a small brown-and-white creature with floppy ears. It barked and shit everywhere and chewed up any shoes left on the floor. But everyone else thought it was wonderful, cute and cuddly. Tommy named it Fuzz Ball.

The gerbils were kept in their own room, with an old blanket that McAllister wearily ordered to be torn into strips. The gerbils then finished the job. Unlike the puppy, which had to be coaxed to eat mashed-up soy and only did so when it got hungry enough, the gerbils ate the vegetable crops happily. But their room smelled and had to be cleaned out every day, and Pete couldn't see the point of them.

"Wait," McAllister said. "Something is going to happen, I think."

"What?" Pete said.

"I don't know."

"Is it because of what I saw?"

"I really don't know."

She didn't seem to know much. And once, Pete had thought she knew everything!

Two of the gerbils died the day after Caity brought them back. Pete hoped the rest would die, too, and maybe even the puppy, but they didn't. The gerbils ate and smelled, the puppy raced around and barked and chewed, the babies wailed.

"A regular madhouse, this," Darlene muttered.

Ravi went on a Grab and returned with yet another large load of objects on yet another large rolling cart. "Look! Look what I got!"

Bundles of tough, heavy cloth that Pete thought would be poor blankets: too uncomfortable. However, it turned out they were not blankets at all. Eduardo let out a whoop such as Pete had never before heard the quiet man make. Eduardo sat on the floor and did things to one of the bundles and it sprang into a little cloth *room*.

"A tent!" Tommy cried, and crawled inside.

McAllister leaned against the wall, her hand on her belly, and stared at the "tent."

Eduardo said to McAllister, "Five-pole four-season Storm King. An earlier generation of these is what we used to use on field expeditions in the mountains, when I was a grad student in botany." Pete didn't know what a botany or a grad student were, and he didn't ask. He was too jealous.

There were more tents, plus a lot of rope, a sharp "axe" that McAllister immediately took away some-place, and many metal things Pete didn't understand the use of. McAllister directed it all to be stowed back on the rolling cart—no playing with this one—and pulled into the room next to the gerbils.

But the most interesting thing, McAllister didn't see at all. Ravi said quietly to Pete, "Come with me. I want to show you something."

"I can't leave the Grab room. I'm next." Pete already wore the wrister.

"Then wait until everybody leaves."

Pete nodded, although he wasn't sure he wanted to see anything from Ravi. Pete regarded it as a private triumph that when he masturbated he no longer thought of McAllister; now he imagined the beautiful red-haired girl that had been Susie's big sister. He'd already calculated how many years before Susie herself would be ready for sex. Still, every time he saw the growing curve of McAllister's belly, the old animosity toward Ravi stirred.

At the same time, he and Ravi were now allies. Together they were going to get revenge for Earth. The first Tesslie they saw—and one had to show up eventually, after all he'd seen one when he'd gone Outside!—they were going to kill. They spent a lot of time in Pete's clear-walled secret room, gazing out at the growing grasses in the black rock and planning ways to accomplish this. If the Tesslie was an alien inside a bucket-case they could hit the case with something until it cracked open, drag the alien out, and stomp on it. If it was a robot, they would find the batteries and pull them out.

"Look," Ravi said when everyone else had left the Grab room. He reached under his tunic, made from a thick blanket folded and sewn to create pockets. Ravi pulled out something encased in leather. The leather slipped off and there was the knife, long and gleaming and, Pete knew without testing it, really sharp. Then another one.

"They had a lot of knives in the store and I put some on the rolling cart. But these two are for us."

"Yes," Pete said. He took one. Just holding it made him feel strange: powerful and bad, both. But he liked the feeling.

"Yes," he said again.

JULY 2014

JULIE TRIED TO BE GOOD at running and hiding, but most of the time she felt like a fool. After all, she didn't even know if whichever agency had arrested Fanshaw would come for her. And what if they did? All she had done was work on data he had given her.

Data that she knew had been obtained illegally, which made her at the very least an accessory to crime. Data that might, in fact, constitute a terrorist risk.

So why hadn't she reported Fanshaw? Because he must have gotten the data from some government agency, which meant they were already aware of the threat. She couldn't have helped any, and she might have endangered herself. Material witnesses could be detained by the FBI or CIA indefinitely, in secret and without filed charges. If that had happened, who would have cared for Alicia? Linda had her hands full with her job and her own family; Jake was out of the question.

It was because of Alicia that Julie was trying to plan responsibly now. At first light she packed the car carefully. She stopped at the bank as soon as it opened and withdrew $3,000 in cash. She turned off her cell phone. Then she drove north from D.C. on I-270. In Pennsylvania, just over the border from Maryland, she found a seedy motel that looked like it would accept cash. It did. The bored clerk behind a shield of bullet-proof glass didn't check the parking lot to see if the false license number she put down matched the one on her car. If the clerk was surprised to see a woman with a baby walk in to his establishment, which usually catered to an entirely different sort of trade, he didn't show it.

Locking the motel door behind her, Julie had a moment of panic. What was she doing? Her life had been going so well, had felt so sweet—

She was doing what she had to do.

After feeding Alicia, Julie drove to the nearest library and used their Internet connection until the library closed. It helped that Alicia, an unusually good baby now that the first bouts of colic were over, slept peacefully in her infant seat or stared calmly at whatever crossed her vision. Back in her motel room, Julie worked on her own laptop, which couldn't have accessed the Internet if she'd wanted to; this was not the sort of place with Wi-Fi.

When she couldn't go any further with the data she had, she watched the TV. It only got three channels, but that was enough. Through the thin walls came first loud music and then louder laughter, followed by a lot of sexual moaning. Sleep came late and hard. Julie upped the volume on the TV, flipping channels to find what she sought.

"Dead zones" were increasing in the world's oceans. No fish, no algae, no life.

The Nile was threatened by industrial pollution. No fish, no algae, no life.

CO_2 levels in the atmosphere were creeping upward.

Overfishing was causing starvation in Southeast Asian islands.

The noise from adjoining rooms grew louder. A door slammed, hard. Julie's gun, a snub-nosed .38, lay on the floor beside her bed. Julie was licensed to carry, and a reasonably good shot. She didn't expect to have to use the gun, but it was comforting to know she had it.

2035

PETE SAT in the Grab room, waiting for the platform to brighten. He had been there each day for a week now, relieved from duty only to sleep, and he was terrifically bored. Darlene had brought him onions and peppers to slice and chop. Eduardo had brought him sewing. Tommy popped in and out, too restless to stay very long. Caity had strolled in, nonchalantly offering sex, and had stalked out, her back stiff, when Pete said no. Jenna brought Petra, both of them trundled in on the rolling cart by Terrell. Petra was just learning to walk. Pete and Jenna sat a few paces apart and set the baby to waddling happily between them until she got tired and went to sleep.

But most of the time he was bored. Of the Shell's six books, two of them too hard for Pete, and he'd read the others over and over. He knew all about the Cat in the Hat, the fairy tales with all the princes and horses and swords, the moon you said good-night to, and *Animals in the Friendly Zoo*. Why didn't the fucking Grab machinery brighten?

It was a relief of sorts to think bad words, so he said them again, this time aloud. "Why doesn't the fucking Grab machinery brighten?"

"Language, Pete," McAllister said. She smiled at him from the doorway, walked heavily to his side, and braced one hand on the wall to lower herself beside him. Pete blushed, then scowled, conscious of the forbidden knife under his shirt. He had sounded out the words on its sheath: CAUTION: CARLTON HUNTING KNIFE. VERY SHARP.

"I came to keep you company," McAllister said. "Are you very bored?"

"Yes."

"You're doing a good job. You always do."

Pete looked away. He used to love McAllister's praise, used to practically live for it. Now, however, he wondered if she really meant it, or if she just wanted him to keep on doing what she wished. Did she praise all the Six the same way? And the older Grab kids, too?

McAllister watched him carefully. Finally she said, "You're growing up, Pete."

"I am grown up! I'm fifteen!"

"So you are."

Silence, which lengthened until Pete felt he had to say something. "How is the fetus?"

To his surprise, McAllister smiled, and the smile had a tinge of sadness in it. "Doing fine. Do you know how odd it would have been for a fifteen-year-old to utter that sentence, in Before?"

He didn't know. He said belligerently, "I don't see why. That fetus is important to us."

"You're right. And you Six have all grown up knowing that. Language follows need. It was your father who taught me that, you know. He was studying to be a linguist."

Startlement shook Pete out of his belligerence. McAllister—none of the Survivors—talked much about the ones who had died, or about their own lives Before. When he'd been a child, Pete and the other Six had asked hundreds of questions, which always received the same answer: "Now is what counts, now and the future." Caity had pointed out, years ago, that the Survivors must have made a pact to say that. Gradually everyone had stopped asking.

Now Pete said carefully (*CAUTION: VERY SHARP*), "My father?"

"Yes. Richard had been a student at the same university I was, although we didn't know each other then."

"Where was that?" This flow of information was unprecedented. Pete didn't want to ask anything complicated that might interrupt it.

"The name of the university wouldn't mean anything to you, and there's no reason why it should. That's all gone, and what matters is now and the future."

"Yes, of course, but how did my father get here, McAllister? How did you?"

She sighed and shifted uncomfortably on the floor. Pete tried to imagine carrying something the size of a bucket inside you. McAllister said, "I was home from university for summer vacation when the Tesslie destruction began. They caused a megatsunami. That's a... You've seen waves in the ocean when you've been on a Grab, right? A tsunami is a wave so huge it was higher than the whole Shell, and could wash it right away. Wash away whole cities. The Tesslies started the tsunami with an earthquake in the Canary Islands off the coast of Europe and it rolled west across the Atlantic."

Her face had changed. Pete thought: *She's talking to herself now, not me*, but he didn't mind as long as she kept talking. He'd never seen McAllister like this. Was it because she was pregnant? It had been a while since anyone in the Shell had been pregnant: at least six years, when Bridget had miscarried that last time. The Survivors were too old (or so everyone had thought) and the Grab kids too young. The Shell was awash in babies, but in the last years no pregnancies. Until now.

McAllister kept talking, her back resting against the Grab room wall, her hands resting lightly on the mound of her belly. "We lived, my family and I, in the countryside of southern Maryland. Honeysuckle and mosquitoes. Dad had a little tobacco farm that had been in the family for generations. Ten acres, two barns, a house built by my great-grandfather. It wasn't very profitable but he liked the life. We had no close neighbors. That day my parents drove my little brother to Baltimore for a doctor's appointment, a specialist. Jimmy had had leukemia but he was recovering well. I woke up late and turned on the little TV in my room while I was getting dressed and I learned that by then the tsunami was forty-five minutes away. My parents might have been trying to call me but I'd forgotten to plug in my cell and the battery was dead."

The words made no sense to Pete but he didn't interrupt her.

"Mom and Dad had taken our only car—we didn't have much money and I was at university on a merit scholarship. They were so proud of that. I ran out of the house and climbed the hill behind the barns. The hill wasn't very high, not in coastal Virginia, but it was high enough to see the water coming. A huge wall of it, smashing everything, trees and houses and tobacco barns. *Our* house. I knew it was going to smash me."

Pete blurted, despite himself, "What did you do?"

To his surprise, she chuckled. "I prayed. For the first time in a decade—I was a smart-ass college kid who thought she had outgrown all that hooey—I prayed to a god, any god, to save me. And then a Tesslie did. It materialized out of the air beside me in what looked like a shower of golden sparks—that's why we called them Tesslies, you know. Ted Mgambe came up with the name. He said when they materialized through whatever unthinkable machinery they had, it looked just like the shower of sparks from Tesla's famous experiments."

She had gone beyond Pete again. He didn't interrupt.

"The materializing was quite a trick, but the Tesslie was solid enough, a hard-shelled space suit, or perhaps a robot, with flexible long tentacles. It wrapped one around me but it really didn't have to. The tsunami was almost on me, a wall of dirty raging water with trees and boards and pieces of cars and even a dead *cow* in it. I saw that cow and I clutched the Tesslie with every ounce of strength I had."

Silence. Pete said, "And then what? What?"

McAllister shrugged. "I woke up in the Shell, along with twenty-five other people. All about my age, all intelligent, all healthy. You know their names. Everything was here except the Grab machinery, which just *appeared* twenty years later when it became evident that we were not going to be able to produce enough children to restart the human race. Too much genetic damage, Xiaobo thought, although nobody knew from what. All of us Survivors came from Maryland and Virginia, although we represented genetic diversity. Xiaobo was a Chinese exchange student, Eduardo was Hispanic, Ted was black, Darlene was plucked from up-country Piedmont. The diversity was probably deliberate. And we all happened to be in the open, high up, and alone when the tsunami hit.

"When each of us regained consciousness, we explored the Shell, and we saw what Earth had become through the clear patch of wall in the unused maze—no, Pete, you weren't the first to go there. And after the initial grief and rage, we made a pact that we would do whatever it took to restart humanity. Anything, anything at all, putting the good of the whole first and our individual selves second, if at all."

"Didn't you hate them? The Tesslies, I mean?"

"Of course we did. They wrecked the world. Even the brief hysterical newscast I saw that last day said that the tsunami wasn't natural. It came from something—a quake, a volcano, I don't remember exactly—that couldn't have happened in that way by itself. And then the Tesslies saved us, like lab rats. We expected biological experimentation on us, those first years. It didn't happen. The Tesslies left us alone until they gave us the Grab machinery, although no one saw them do it. Until you went Outside, I thought they'd probably left Earth for good. But they hadn't, and I think now that they're here for whatever happens next. Because something *is* happening, Pete. The grass is growing Outside. You breathed the air, even if it isn't completely right yet. The Grabs have accelerated enormously. It's possible more Tesslies will return soon."

"Before, did you—"

She held out her hand. "Give me the knife, Pete. Or the gun, or whatever you've got."

He jerked his head to face her. His body shifted away. "No."

"Please. You can't do any good with it."

All at once fury swamped him in a big wave, like the tsunami she had spoken about but evidently didn't understand. None of them understood anything, the wimpy Survivors! He shouted, "What's wrong with you, McAllister? What? The Tesslies wrecked my future! Everybody's future! And you want to just welcome them back because they gave us the Shell and the Grabs and—when the Grab machinery appeared it didn't even have any learning circle to teach you that adults can't go through and so we lost Robert and Seth until that day Ravi jumped on it during a game and it happened to brighten and he came back whole! And still you never blame the Tesslies, you never blame anybody for anything, you just talk about the good of the whole but to not blame the Tesslies—Fuck, fuck, fuck! Do you hear me? Fuck! We're not...not gerbils!"

"No. But you're not thinking clearly, either. Survival—"

"Blame the fucking Tesslies! Hate them! Kill them if you can!"

"Pete—"

The platform brightened.

Pete pulled his knife, glared at the pregnant woman on the floor, and jumped into the Grab.

JULY 2014

THE YELLOWSTONE caldera lifted upwards.

For several years the surface land had been rising as much as three inches a year, but a few years ago the uplift had slowed and stopped. Now the ground inched upward again. A swarm of minor earthquakes followed, barely detectable at the surface. Tourists went on admiring the geysers and the bubbling, mud-laden hot springs. Rumbling at low sonic frequencies set off alarms at the Yellowstone Volcano Observatory and the White Lake GPS station.

Jacob Kahn rushed to his monitor. "Oh my God," he said. It was not a prayer.

JULY 2014

TWO MORE NIGHTS in cheap motels, one without AC in a sweltering July. Two more days on library Internet connections. On her own laptop Julie had run and rerun algorithms as new data became available. Her driving had taken her steadily north, along the coast. Now she was in Massachusetts, north of Salem. She knew where she was going. She had accumulated enough data points to be sure.

The Eve's Garden break-in in Connecticut.

The baby snatched on the Massachusetts coast while her teenage sister slept in the same room.

The Loving Pets burglary in New Hampshire.

Thefts at REI in southern Maine and Whole Foods in Vermont.

She was running out of money, and not all her news-watching had turned up the slightest hint that anyone was looking for her. On the other hand, neither had she turned up any more information on Dr. Fanshaw or mutated plant-killing bacteria. Both the glory hound and the deadly mutation seemed to have vanished, which was in itself scary. Still, she would have to go home soon. Or go somewhere.

Alicia had a cold, probably from exposure to all the germs in all the libraries. Julie had a massive headache. Was she just being stupid, imagining herself some dramatic fugitive from a third-rate action movie? Maybe she was just as narcissistic as Geoffrey Fanshaw. The sensible thing was to make the observation, alert Gordon, and go home.

At a Kmart she bought a camcorder. Alicia sneezed and fussed. Julie got them both back in the hot car and drove north on Route 1. The algorithm pinpointed a Maine town, Port Allington, for the next incident. Also a time: between 5:30 and 5:45 tomorrow afternoon. Which was odd, since all the other incidents had occurred in the middle of the night or in early morning. Google Earth showed the location to be in a retail area centered on a large Costco.

She spent nearly the last of her money at a Ramada Inn, several steps up from the places she'd been staying. "You're lucky to get a room at all," the desk clerk told her. "It's high season for tourists, you know. But we had a cancellation."

"Oh," Julie said. She was tired, headachy, frightened. Alicia fussed in her car seat.

"Tomorrow the Azalea Festival begins over in Cochranton. You here for the festival?"

"No."

"You should go. My niece Meg is going to be crowned Miss Cochranton Azalea."

"Congratulations."

"You should give the festival a look-see."

It took Julie a long time to get to sleep. Her theory—*fanciful, dumb, insane*—kept spinning around in her head. When she finally slept, she dreamed that Miss Cochranton Azalea, dressed in a pink prom dress covered with blossoms, said, "That's the stupidest idea I ever heard. I thought you were supposed to be a scientist!"

The next morning she felt even worse. But today would end it. She fed Alicia, bathed her, had an overcooked breakfast at a Howard Johnson's. It was after noon when she got on the road. Another sweltering day. During just the short walk from restaurant to car, sweat sprang out on Julie's forehead and her sundress clung to her skin. Alicia, in just a diaper and thin yellow shirt, cried while Julie strapped her into her car seat. Julie turned on the AC and powered down the windows to flush the hot air from the car.

Only a few hours to drive, and it would be over.

All at once loneliness overtook her. She hadn't talked to anyone but motel clerks, librarians, and waitresses in days, and you couldn't call any of those things conversations. She felt near to tears. Ordinarily she despised weakness—she and Gordon had had that in common—but the way she'd been living wasn't human. And what did it matter if she turned on her cell? In a few hours the camcorder would have her proof, and she doubted that the FBI or CIA or whoever—even if they were looking for her—could locate her that fast if she were on the road. She needed to talk to somebody. Not Linda, who would ask too many questions. She would call her brother. Not to say anything personal—she and Jake seldom did that—but just to hear his voice.

The phone had nine voice mails waiting.

Sitting in the Howard Johnson's parking lot, the AC finally making the car bearable, Julie stared at the blinking "9." Very few people had this number; she'd conducted her professional life on the more secure landline. Gordon? Had the investigation reopened?

Her fingers shook as she keyed to voice mail.

"Julie, this is Jake. Listen, are you due for vacation? If so, don't travel out west. Nowhere near Yellowstone, do you hear me? I'll call and explain more when I have a minute to think clearly."

A mechanical voice informed her that the message was dated days ago, the day Julie had left D.C. The next message was also from Jake, a day later: "Sorry to alarm you, Sis, but my warning still holds. Some weird shit is happening here, signs that the Yellowstone Caldera could blow. You remember, don't you, I told you that for years now it's been ranked 'high threat'? Well, I guess it'll rank that way a while longer since nothing seems to be happening even though there's enough magma down there to blow up the entire state. Well, several states, actually. But as I said, it seems to have settled down. But don't come out here until you hear from me."

The next message alternated between jocularity and exasperation. "Still no supervolcano at Yellowstone. Just call us at the U.S. Geological Survey a bunch of Cassandras. But why haven't you phoned me? This is my third message."

Five of the other messages were from Linda, one from the hairdresser announcing that Julie had missed her appointment. Linda, calling first from home and then from Winnipeg, sounded increasingly frantic: "Where *are* you? It's not like you to not call me back." Her last message said she was calling the police.

Julie keyed in Linda's number, but it went to voice mail. Were the police already looking for her as a missing person? No, that last message was only an hour ago. Julie left Linda a voice mail saying she was fine, Alicia was fine, tell the police it was all a mistake, Julie would explain later.

Almost she smiled, imagining that explanation.

She pulled out and drove toward Port Allington.

JULY 2014

THE ALARMS CAME from the Canary Islands station, simultaneously sounding at the Consejo Superior de Investigaciones Científicas offices in Madrid and Barcelona, and then around the world.

"La Palma!" a graduate student in Barcelona exclaimed. "It's breaking off!"

"Not possible," her superior said sharply. "That old computer model was disproved—you should know that! You mean El Teide!" He raced to the monitors.

It was not El Teide, the world's third-largest volcano, which had been smoldering on Tenerife for decades. It was the island of La Palma. A massive landslide of rock from Cumbre Vieja, itself already split in half and fissured from a 1949 earthquake, broke off the mountain. One and a half million cubic feet of rock fell into the Atlantic as the earth shook and split. The resulting tsunami crested at nearly 2,000 feet, engulfing the islands. The landslide continued underwater and a second quake followed. More crests and troughs were generated, creating a wave train.

"Not possible," the volcanologist choked out again. "The model—"

The ground shook in Barcelona.

The wave train sped west out to sea.

JULY 2014

It WASN'T DARK, and it wasn't light, until it was. Pete blinked. No Grab before had gone like this.

He stood in a vast store, bigger than any he'd ever seen. WELCOME TO COSTCO! said a huge red sign. The lights were full on. The big doors just behind him stood wide open. But there were no people in the store, and none of the Before cars in what he could see of the parking lot. Everything was completely silent. A few tables had been tipped over, and half-full shopping carts stood everywhere.

"Hello?" Pete said, but very softly. He held Ravi's knife straight out in front of him. No one answered.

Cold slid down Pete, from his crooked shoulder on down his spine right to the tops of his legs. But he wasn't here to give in to fear, or to start conversations with weirdly absent people. He was here to Grab. He took one of the half-filled shopping carts—part of his job already done!—and pushed it past a display of round black tires. Not useful. Behind it were tables and tables of clothes, and behind those he could see furniture and food. What would McAllister want most?

As he pushed a shopping cart forward, something miraculous came into view: an entire wall of DIGITAL

FOTO FRAMES. But these were enormous, and the pictures on them *moved*. In each DIGITAL FOTO FRAME a beautiful girl, more beautiful even than Susie's red-haired older sister, ran along a white beach and into blue sparkling water. The girl wore almost no clothes, just strips of bright cloth around her hips and breasts. The breasts bounced. Mouth open, Pete stared at the incredible sight. Could he maybe unfasten one from the wall and—

He heard a clatter behind him and he turned.

JULY 2014

SOMETHING WAS WRONG. Suddenly cars jammed the exits to Route 1, as if everyone was trying to leave the highway at once. Julie would have guessed a massive accident blocking traffic, except that the cars were leaving the freeway in both directions. Could a wreck ahead be sprawled across all six lanes? Or maybe a fire? She didn't see smoke in the hot blue sky. She turned on the radio.

"—as high as 150 feet when it reaches the coast of the United States! Citizens are urged not to panic. Turn your radio to the National Emergency Alert System and follow orderly evacuation procedures. The tsunami will not hit for another four hours. Repeat, the Canary Islands tsunami will not hit the eastern seaboard of the United States for another four hours. Turn to the National Emergency Alert System—"

Tsunami. Waves 150 feet high hitting the coast of the United States.

For a moment Julie's vision blurred. The car wavered slightly, but only slightly. She recovered herself—Alicia was with her. She had to save Alicia. Drive inland—

She couldn't get off the highway. Traffic had slowed

to a crawl, fighting for the exit ramps. An SUV left the highway and drove fast and hard into the fence separating the wide shoulder from a row of suburban houses. The fence broke. A blue Ford followed the SUV.

She knew about the "Canary Islands tsunami"—it had been the subject of a melodramatic TV show. Jake had discussed with her just why the program was wrong. "It couldn't happen that way, Sis. The fault isn't big enough, it was exaggerated for the computer model. And the model was based on algorithms— you'll appreciate this—used for undersea linear quakes, not single-point events. It's pure and inaccurate sensationalism. You would need a major seabed reconfiguration to get that megatsunami. Or an atomic bomb set off underwater."

Hands shaking on the wheel, Julie pulled her car off the highway and followed the blue Ford toward the fence. She had to drive down a slight incline and through a watery ditch, but her wheels didn't get stuck in the mud and the ground past the ditch was firm and hard, although covered with weeds. Her door handles and fenders tore off the tallest of these. Festooned with Queen Anne's lace, the car drove through the fence hole and across somebody's back yard. It was an old-fashioned 1950s house with a separate garage. Julie followed the two cars around the garage, down the driveway, and onto a road.

Everybody here was driving west, away from the ocean. But Julie had had time to think. Inland was not the answer. Not to the whole picture.

Her hands shook on the wheel as, guided by the compass on her dash display, she turned east. For several blocks she had to fight cars dashing out of driveways, the people glimpsed through windshields looking frantic and shocked. Cars jumped lanes, blocking her way. A woman stuck her head out of the window and screamed at Julie, "Hey! You're going the wrong way!"

By the edge of town, however, she had the road nearly to herself. No one else was heading toward the sea.

How far inland would the evacuees have to go to escape the tsunami? Jake had once told her that 8,000 years ago in the Norwegian sea, an ancient rockslide had left sediment fifty miles into Scotland.

With one hand she fiddled with the radio, searching for more information. A Canadian station broke off its broadcast to say something about the Yellowstone Caldera, then abruptly went off the air.

In her car seat, Alicia slept fitfully.

In Washington, in Brasilia, in Delhi, in London, in Pyongyang, in Moscow, in Beijing, the Canary Islands earthslide was perceived as unnatural. Too large, too sudden, in the wrong place, not the result of natural plate tectonics. Every single country had received the data on the quake and resulting tsunami. Every single country had a classified file describing the feasibility and techniques for using nuclear blasts at Cumbre Vieja as a weapon. Every single country came to the same conclusion.

In Washington the president, his family, and senior staff were airlifted to an undisclosed location. From the chopper he could see the Beltway with its murderous fight to get out of D.C. Most would not make it. He could see the dome of Capitol Hill, the Washington Monument, the Smithsonian with its treasures, the gleaming terraces of the Kennedy Center and mellow rosy brick of Georgetown. All would be gone in a few more hours.

"I need more information," he said to his chief of staff.

"Sir, retaliation scenarios are in place for—"

"I need more information."

A woman stood in the doorway of the store, carrying a sort of padded bucket with a handle, curved to hold a baby. The baby was asleep. The woman and Pete stared at each other. She spoke first.

"You're the one who has been stealing children, aren't you?"

"Not stealing," Pete said. "Rescuing."

"From the tsunami."

It was the second time Pete had heard that word today. He scowled to cover his confusion. "No. From the Tesslies."

"What are Tesslies?" She moved closer, just one step. It was as if she were pulled closer, jerked on some string Pete couldn't see, like the puppets Bridget had made for the Six when they were kids. The woman looked about McAllister's age, although not so pretty. Her hair matted to her scalp and her clothing was wet over her breasts, which made Pete look away. He started throwing bundles of towels into a shopping cart.

"You're taking things from this store, the way you did from the others. A sporting-goods store in Maine. A pet store in New Hampshire. A garden shop in Connecticut. A supermarket in Vermont. Ambler's Family Department Store in Connecticut..."

She recited the whole list of store Grabs, his and Caity's and Ravi's and Terrell's and Paolo's and even way back to Jenna's famous Wal-Mart Grab. Pete stopped hurling towels into the cart and stared at her, astonished. "How do you know all that? Who told you?"

"Nobody told me, or at least not all of it. A law enforcement joint task force that... No, it would take too long to explain. You aren't here for long, are you? How much longer?"

Automatically Pete glanced at the wrister. "Sixteen more minutes."

"I've been waiting outside for you."

More astonishment. "You have? Why? Don't try to stop me!"

"I won't stop you. At first I came to video you, to get photographic proof that... It doesn't matter. That's not why I'm here now. Listen to me, please— what's your name?"

"Pete." He yanked at another shopping cart and started emptying a table of clothing into it. So much clothing! And most of it big enough for Ravi and the Survivors. Eduardo's pants had a hole in them.

"My name is Julie. Listen to me, Pete. The tsunami will be here within the hour. It will smash everything on the eastern coast of the United States. Almost no one will survive—"

"McAllister will. She told me." Pants, tops, jackets, more pants but softer. "All the Survivors will live."

"Yes? Where will they go?"

"The Tesslies will take them to the Shell."

"That's where you live, the Shell? Where is it?"

"After." A third shopping cart. If he could tie them together, they would all come back with him—a lot more than Ravi had Grabbed! Better stuff, too. He yanked free a towel to lash the carts together.

"But the Shell is a safe place, isn't it? Is it some sort of space ship or underground colony? Are you from the future? It—oh my God!"

At her voice, Pete jumped. She stared at the wall behind him. He whirled around to look, knife at the ready. If it was a Tesslie—

JULY 2014

THE FRONT WAVE of the megatsunami loomed 300 feet high when it crashed into northwest Africa. When it reached the low-lying south coast of England, the trough of the wave hit first. The sea retreated in a long, eerie drawback before rushing back to land. It breached England's sea defenses, roaring a mile inland, destroying everything it touched.

The main body of the wave train sped over the Atlantic at hundreds of miles per hour. When eventually it reached Brazil, the Caribbean, Florida, and the eastern coast of the United States, it would crest to a maximum of 120 feet.

Long before that, the missiles had been launched. Retaliation for the act of terrorism aimed at smashing the way of life of the Western world. The counter-response was not far behind.

The far wall of huge DIGITAL FOTO FRAME had stopped showing the moving pictures of the beautiful girl running on the beach. Instead, they all showed fire spurting into the sky. At the same moment the ground shook beneath Pete's feet and he nearly fell. The woman staggered sideways against a table of rugs, righted herself, stared again at the row of DIGITAL

FOTO FRAMES, which were screaming loud enough now to wake the baby. Something about a yellow stone.

Julie said, in a voice Pete recognized: "There goes the West. To match the East." The words made no sense, but the voice was the one Bridget had used when her last baby miscarried. Quiet, toneless, dead.

Pete stared at this baby, now awake in its padded bucket and peering curiously around. Was it a girl? How hard would Julie fight for it?

She said, "Take us with you."

He gaped at her. She didn't give him a chance to speak.

"You can, I know you can. You've taken twelve children, starting—"

"Thirteen," he corrected, without thinking.

"—with Tommy Candless over a year ago, and you can take us. Don't you understand, Pete? Everything here is dying, the Earth itself is dying! Tsunamis, earthquakes, a mutated bacteria that is killing every plant above tide level. Governments will collapse, and as they collapse they'll fight back, there will be nuclear retaliation with radiation that will—"

"Radiation, yes." She had used a word he knew. "It damages babies. It damaged me. But it's mostly gone now."

"Is it? Then take—"

"Everything you said, the destroying of the whole Earth—the *Tesslies* did that. But McAllister is leading us to restart humanity. And Ravi and I will kill the fucking alien Tesslies!"

"The—"

Suddenly all the DIGITAL FOTO FRAMES went black at once. The silence somehow felt loud. Into it Julie said, "No aliens wrecked the Earth. We did. Humans."

"That's a lie!"

"No, Pete, it's not. We poisoned the Earth and raped her and denuded her. We ruined the oceans and air and forests, and now she is fighting back."

"The Tesslies destroyed the world!"

"I don't think so. Tell me this: Are there any plants where you live? Growing wild outside the Shell, I mean?"

"There are now. Grasses and bushes and red flowers."

Julie closed her eyes, and her lips moved soundlessly. When she opened her eyes again, they were wet. "Thank God. Or Gaia. The microbial mutation reversed."

"What?"

"Take us with you, Pete. I can help your McAllister start over. I'm strong and a good worker and I know a lot of different things. I can be really useful to...to the Shell."

She took a step forward and looked at him with such beseeching eyes that all at once Pete *saw* her. She was a real person, as real as McAllister or Petra or Ravi, a person who was going to die in McAllister's tsunami. The first person in Before who had ever been real to him.

"Take us with you!"

He choked out, "I can't!"

"Yes, you can! You've done it twelve times already!"

"Only kids," Pete said. "If adults go through a Grab, they die." Robert, Seth, the thing that had come back with him and Kara and Petra. The thing that had been their father. "The Tesslies made the Grab that way. They didn't want the Survivors to just get everybody on the platform and lead them all back to Before."

Julie went so still and so sick-looking that for a crazy moment Pete thought she had turned into the "yellow stone" the wall had been screaming about. *Robert, Seth, the thing that had been Petra's father...* He started to babble. "But I can take that baby, yes I can, kids can go through a Grab so I can take the baby! Give it to me!"

Julie didn't move.

"Give me the baby! I've only got—" a quick glance at his wrister "—another two and a half minutes!"

The number brought her alive. She shoved the baby bucket into his arms. "Her name is Alicia. Tell her—oh, tell her about me!"

"Okay." He couldn't do that; it was important that the Grab kids belong to the Shell, not to Before. McAllister insisted on it. But he didn't have to tell Julie that.

She began to cry. Pete hated it when people cried. But she had a good reason, and anyway there were only three or four sobs before she got hold of herself and began to talk. "Listen, Pete, it *was* us, not any aliens. Have you ever heard of Gaia?"

"No."

"Is your McAllister an educated man?"

"She knows everything."

"Then tell her this: *We did it*. We wrecked the Earth, and now the Earth is fighting back. The planet is full of self-regulating mechanisms—remember those exact words!—to keep life intact. We've violated them, and Gaia—remember that word!—is cleansing herself of us. It's not mysticism, it's Darwinian self-preservation. Maybe Gaia will start over. Maybe you in the Shell are part of that! But tell McAllister that, tell everyone! Say it!"

She was hysterical, the way Petra's mother had got hysterical when Pete Grabbed Petra. But she was also real. So Pete repeated the words after her, and then repeated them again, all the while hurling more things into shopping carts. "Gaia. Darwinian self-preservation." Blankets, socks, a tableful of flimsy books. "Self-regulating planetary mechanisms." Three folding chairs, all he had room for. "Identical deadly plant mutations in widely separated places. Gaia." Now he'd reached the start of the food section. Loaves of bread! Boxes of something else!

The ground shook again. The baby started to whimper. Pete tied the huge shopping carts together with towels. He clutched one of the handles in one hand, the baby bucket in the other. Fifteen seconds.

"Bye, Julie. I'm sorry about the tsunami."

"Alicia!" Julie cried. Then, stopping herself in mid-lunge: "It was us."

"It was the Tesslies."

"No, no—don't you see? We humans always blame the wrong ones! The—"

Pete never heard the rest. He was Grabbed.

2035

"I'M BACK!" Pete cried from the platform. "Look! Look!" No one was in the Grab room.

That made no sense. McAllister had seen him go. She knew he would be back in twenty-two minutes, and his wrister said that he was. She, at least, should be waiting here. Disappointment lurched through him—he had a baby girl to show her! And all this great stuff! And all those words to tell her that Julie had said... If he could remember them.

He found he remembered them perfectly.

Pete's belly churned. The excitement of the Grab, the disappointment at no one seeing his triumphant return, his deep disturbance at Julie's statements, going deeper every moment. Where was McAllister? Where was everybody?

"Hello?" he said, but not loud. No answer.

He hopped off the platform, leaving his Grabbed prizes, still carrying Alicia in her baby-bucket. Cautiously he peered into the corridor.

No one. But through the wide arched entrance to the farm, he glimpsed a movement behind the wide white bulk of the fertilizer machine. A second later

Ravi appeared, gestured wildly for Pete to come, then ducked again out of sight. Was it a game of some sort?

He knew it wasn't. He set the baby-bucket down in the middle of the corridor and sprinted toward Ravi.

"We don't have much time," Ravi gasped. "They'll find out it's missing. My knife doesn't work at all on its bucket-case. But you have the laser on your wrister. Quick, kill it!"

Lying on the ground at Ravi's feet was a Tesslie.

JULY 2014

JULIE WALKED CALMLY to a deep faux-leather chair in the Costco furniture display. Calmly she sat down. The calm, she knew with the part of her brain that was still rational, would not last. It was shock. Also several other things, including a preternaturally heightened ability to simultaneously comprehend everything around her, instead of in the linear shards that the human mind was usually stuck with.

Alicia was gone.

The megatsunami was on its way.

Washington D.C., including her life there, would soon no longer exist.

Her country would not allow that to go by without a military reaction.

Pete had left behind a pile of objects that must have slid off one of his shopping carts before he…left.

Jake was dead in whatever was happening at the Yellowstone Caldera.

The TVs on the wall had stopped broadcasting.

The Tokyo earthquake and tsunami had been a rehearsal for what would come, once the biologists had detected and contained the plant mutations. Or, alternatively, once Gaia had changed its tactics.

The chair she sat in was on sale for $179.99.

Linda and her family were in Winnipeg, far from the coast. Would that save them? For how long? Gordon and his kids, all the people Julie knew at Georgetown and in D.C.—all gone, or soon to be gone. And then incongruously: *The motel clerk's niece will never be crowned Miss Cochranton Azalea.*

Julie drew the snub-nosed .38 from her pocket. She would not wait for the tsunami. This was better. And Alicia—her baby, her treasure, the miracle she had given up hoping to have—was safe. Safe someplace that might, with any luck, become the future.

JULY 2014

BENEATH THE YELLOWSTONE Caldera, the geothermal system exploded from pressure from below. A magma pool twenty miles by forty miles blew into the sky, greater than the supervolcano in Indonesia that, 75,000 years ago, had killed fifty percent of the human race. More than 250 cubic miles of magma erupted into the air. For hundreds of miles everything burned, and ash choked the air. Burning, suffocating night spread over the land.

The explosion triggered earthquakes in the San Andreas Fault and on into the Pacific Rim. As convergent tectonic plate boundaries lifted or subducted, more tsunamis were generated in the Pacific, and then in the Indian Ocean. Even deep sea life was affected as thermal vents opened—but not affected very much. Most of the ocean life was hardy, adapted, and innocent.

2035

Pete gaped at the Tesslie lying at Ravi's feet. Or... was it lying? The thing was the squarish metal can he remembered, without clear head or feet or *anything*. He said, inanely, "How do you know it isn't standing up instead of lying down?"

"Because I knocked it over!"

"Did it come out of the air in a bunch of golden sparks?"

"Yes!"

"It's not moving. How do you know it's still alive?"

"It won't be if you fucking laser it!"

Pete didn't move. Ravi leaped forward, grabbed Pete's arm with both hands, and fumbled with the buckle on the wrister.

Ideas surged and eddied in Pete's mind, even as he kept his eyes on the Tesslie. It lay still now, but Pete knew it wasn't helpless. It was watching. Without eyes or anything, it was still watching to see what he and Ravi would do. And it was not helpless. The Tesslies had built this whole Shell! They had made Grab machinery to send the Six back to get kids and stuff! They had come from someplace else through the sky! One of them was not going to let a human laser him open. Ravi was crazy.

But even more, Julie's words swirled in his brain. *"Self-regulating planetary mechanisms." "Darwinian self-preservation." "Gaia." "We did it. We wrecked the Earth."* And *"We humans always blame the wrong ones."*

Pete pushed Ravi away. Ravi said, "What the fuck? Give me the laser."

"I can't."

"You mean you can't laser the bastard? I can! Give it to me, you wimp!"

"I don't know...maybe the Tesslies...I don't know!" It was a cry of anguish. *We humans always blame the wrong ones.*

Ravi, much stronger than Pete, knocked him to the ground and sat on him. Pete stuck his arm with the wrister behind his back. Ravi easily got it out, but he couldn't unbuckle the wrister and also keep both Pete's arms pinned. Pete flailed, wrenching his bad shoulder, hitting Ravi's face, shoulder, anywhere he could reach. Ravi snarled at him, exposing the crooked stumps of the teeth that Pete had knocked out.

The Tesslie turned itself so it stood on a different side of its bucket-case, and waited quietly.

"Give it to me, you wimp!"

"No! McAllister said—"

"It took McAllister! It took them all, you fucking idiot! They're prisoners! That's why I—give it to me!" He smashed a fist into Pete's face.

"Prisoners?" He could barely get the word out for pain, even though he'd turned his head in time for Ravi's blow to hit him on the side of the jaw instead of on the mouth.

"Yes! The bastards took them all!"

"Petra?"

"Give it to me!"

"Took where?"

Ravi flipped Pete over and wrenched his arm behind his head. The pain was astonishing. Ravi got the wrister unbuckled, sprang off Pete, and aimed the laser at the Tesslie. Ravi fired.

Nothing happened.

Pete, gasping on the floor, saw the laser beam hit the Tesslie's bucket-case. The red beam vanished. The Tesslie stood stolid and silent.

Ravi gave a low moan. Pete got to his feet. His vision blurred during the process, but he did it. He faced the Tesslie.

"Don't hurt him, please. He doesn't know. He thinks *you* destroyed everything."

The Tesslie said and did nothing.

Pete blurted, "Did you?"

Nothing.

"Or was it really—" All of a sudden he couldn't remember the weird name Julie had said. Gouda? Or was that the cheese Caity had once brought back from a Grab? Guide-a? Gaga? Gina?

"—us?"

The Tesslie rose a few inches into the air and moved past Pete, floating on nothing at all toward the corridor. A long ropelike metal arm shot out of its tin can, startling Pete. The arm flicked toward him, then pointed to the corridor. The Tesslie floated on, and Pete followed.

"I'm not going!" Ravi shouted. "I'm not!"

"Wimp," Pete said.

In the corridor he picked up Alicia's baby-bucket. She had started to fuss, working up to a full wail. The Tesslie floated on, toward the maze at the far end and then through its small rooms. Pete trailed behind because he needed McAllister and anyway he couldn't think what else to do. What if they were all dead? What if he and this baby were going to their deaths?

That made no sense.

But, then, neither did anything else.

He heard Darlene first. She was singing at the top of her lungs, belting out a desperate stupid song in her scratchy voice: "'Onward, Christian soldiers! Marching as to war...'"

McAllister had told Darlene not to sing that song because wars were all over. Darlene had never listened. Now Pete could hear a baby wailing. Then McAllister's voice, sharp and uncharacteristically angry: "Darlene, stop that!"

Darlene didn't. The Tesslie and Pete rounded a corner in the maze and faced an open door.

They were all crowded into one small room. McAllister and Darlene and Eduardo stood in the front. Behind them huddled Caity, Paolo, Jenna, Terrell. The Grab children were penned in the corner, the babies lying on the bare metal floor. Two more Tesslies guarded the doorway. Pete ran past them to McAllister. "Are you hurt? Is anybody hurt? What happened?"

Caity said, "They brought us here! Like...like gerbils!"

Where *were* the gerbils? Then Pete saw them, trying to get out of a large bucket. They couldn't. Tommy held the squirming Fuzz Ball. Tommy's eyes were big as bucket bottoms.

McAllister said, "You Grabbed another child? Where's Ravi?"

"He—"

The edges of the room began to shimmer with golden sparks.

McAllister ran forward, her big belly swaying. "No, please, not without Ravi—please!"

No response from any of the three Tesslies.

"Please! Listen, we're so grateful for all you've done but if you're really helping us again, we need everyone! We need Ravi!"

"That angel ain't going to listen to you!" Darlene said, with all the bitterness of her bitter self. "Them cherubim are flaming swords! Don't you know nothing?"

"Please," McAllister said to the Tesslie. And then, "Ravi is fertile!"

The golden sparks stopped.

"Ueeuuggthhhg," Caity said, which might have meant anything.

"Flaming swords!" Darlene shouted, and several

children began to cry. McAllister whirled around and slapped Darlene. Pete gaped at McAllister; Darlene put her hand to her red cheek; Caity looked scared in a way that Caity never did; more children screamed.

A fourth Tesslie dragged Ravi into the room, its ropy metal arm wrapped around Ravi's neck. Released, Ravi stumbled forward as if pushed. He fell into Jenna, who also went down with a cry of pain. Jenna's fragile bones—

Pete had no time to pull Ravi off Jenna, or to pick up the crying Alicia, or to clutch at McAllister. The sparks enveloped all of them in a shower of gold, and then there was nothing.

It wasn't dark, and it wasn't light. It wasn't anything except cold. *I'm dead*, Pete thought, but of course he wasn't.

He lay on something hard in places and soft in others. The air felt warm and thick. Something gray shifted above him, far above him. Some noise, faint and rhythmic, sounded over and over in his ears. Something stirred behind him.

The cold retreated abruptly and Pete returned fully to himself. He sprawled Outside, beside Ravi and McAllister, and underneath Ravi was Jenna. He lay *Outside*, partly on rock and partly on some plant low and green and alive. Gray clouds blew overhead. Warm wind ruffled his hair. Dazed, he got to his feet, just as the others began to move.

They were all there, stirring on the ground. The Tesslies were gone. The Shell was gone. Piles of stuff lay on the ground in places where, he vaguely realized, it had all been lying when the Shell enclosed it: toys, blankets, food, tents, piles and piles of buckets. Pete turned around.

This was the view he'd had when he'd gone Outside through the funeral slot and then had gone around to the far side of the Shell. He stood on a high ridge of black rock. Below him the land sloped down to the sea. The whole long slope was a mixture of bare rock, green plants, red flowery bushes. A brownish river gushed down the hillside. Beyond, along the shore, the land flattened and gold-and-green plants grew more thickly a long way out, until the water began.

It was quiet Eduardo who spoke first. "Regenerated from wind-blown seeds, maybe. From...wherever survived. And those lupines are nitrogen-fixers, enriching the soil."

McAllister said shakily, "There must still be ash in the air, it's so thick, but it's breathable...fresh water...." She put her hands over her face, all at once reminding Pete of Julie, in the last-ever Grab.

He didn't want to remember Julie, not now. He wanted to shout, he wanted to cry, he wanted to run down the slope, he wanted to turn around and hit Ravi. He did none of those things. Instead he said, before he was going to do it, a single word. "Gaia."

McAllister jerked her hands away from her face and turned to him sharply. "What?"

"Gaia. It's a word the woman in the Grab said to me. Julie. Alicia's mother." He pointed at Alicia, who was now screaming with the full force of her lungs.

Several other children also began to cry. Pete said some of Julie's other words: "'Self-regulating mechanisms.' 'Planetary Darwinian self-preservation.' 'Cleansing.'"

Eduardo drew a sharp breath. Now the other children were shouting or screaming or whimpering. Fuzz Ball barked and raced around in circles. Darlene started to sing something about Earth abiding. Jenna began to cry. Into the din Pete said, "*We* did it. Not the Tesslies. Us. That's what Julie said."

McAllister didn't answer. She stared out at the water, which wasn't all that bright but still hurt Pete's eyes to look at. He could tell McAllister was thinking, but he couldn't tell what. All at once she turned to look at him, and in her dark eyes he saw something he couldn't name, except that he knew she felt it deeply.

Eduardo said to her, "The Gaia theory... It posited a self-regulating planet to keep conditions optimum for life. A planet that corrects any conditions that might threaten..." He didn't finish.

McAllister said to Pete, "Thank you."

"For what?"

"We'll do better this time."

"Better at what?" Why didn't he ever understand her?

But McAllister turned her beseeching look on Eduardo. "Our chances—"

"I don't know," he said quietly. "Maybe we can. If the seeds take. If any of those grasses are domesticable grains. If enough marine life survived. If we're in a tropical climate. I don't know. Maybe we can."

Can *what?* Before Pete could ask, McAllister's face changed and she was herself again, issuing orders. "Ravi, you and Terrell and Caity and Pete start lugging all that stuff down to that flat, sheltered place by the river—do you see where I mean? Bring the tents first, it's going to rain. And the food, all the food. Darlene, I'm sorry I slapped you. We can discuss it later. For now, try to get rations organized until Eduardo can determine which plants are edible. Eduardo, can you walk enough to find the best spot to put the soy into the ground? Paolo, you and Jenna are going to have to look after all the kids once we get them into tents—I'm sorry, but we can't spare anyone else. Tommy, you help move the food to under cover, and after that I'm going to want you to bring Eduardo some different plants from farther down the slope. Do you think you can do that?"

"Yes!" Tommy beamed at Pete. "You did make a big adventure!"

Pete clutched McAllister's arm. "But I have to finish telling you what Julie—"

"Later," McAllister said. "They'll be time. There will be lots of time."

Pete nodded. He raced with the others to where the Shell had been. The fertilizer machine was gone, the disinfectant and clean-water streams were gone, the Grab machinery was gone. Terrell and Pete each grabbed a rolled-up tent and staggered with it back down the slope. Darlene and Caity lugged buckets of soy stew from what had been the hot part of the farm. Over armfuls of canvas Pete spied Eduardo halfway down the incline to the sea, stooping to examine some low bushy plants.

"'Abide with me,'" Darlene howled. "'The darkness deepens'" until Caity told her to shut the fuck up.

For just a moment, Pete felt afraid. The Shell was all he'd ever known except for the Grabs, those terrifying jolts into places he didn't belong. The Shell had been ugly and boring, but it had been home. Sort of. A cage-sort-of-home. And now—

Had the Tesslies really captured the Survivors, caged them, and twenty years later let them out because the Tesslies wanted to *help?* And what were they, anyway? Robots, aliens, Darlene's angels, rescuers—maybe not even McAllister would ever know.

The moment of fear passed. The Tesslies were gone. This was now. He was here.

A bird swooped overhead, and on the wind came the sweet smell of warm rain.

ACKNOWLEDGMENTS

No book is ever the work of one person. I'd like to thank those who helped make this one possible:

Editor and publisher Jacob Weisman, who made so many valuable suggestions for revision.

Marty Halpern, copyeditor extraordinaire, who not only has one of the sharpest eyes in the business but also understands the difference between copyediting and co-authoring.

Jill Roberts, for her cheerful and prompt emails keeping me in the publishing loop.

And, always, my husband Jack Skillingstead for his encouragement and support.